The Bon Air Boys

The Bon Air Boys Adventure Series

PASSWORD TO
Meade Manor

BY

GREG W. GOLDEN

This book is not intended to endorse or promote any of the activities by the characters contained therein. Any similarity between locations or these characters to actual places or those persons living or dead is coincidental.

This is a fictional story, and although there are elements of actual history herein, it is not intended to be historically accurate.

The Author

PRINTED IN THE UNITED STATES OF AMERICA

Acknowledgments

The inspiration for the stories in this Bon Air Boys series of books came from a time not that long ago. During my late childhood and early teenage years, most moms were homemakers. Television channels arrived through "rabbit ears" on top of the console set that was the focus of most living rooms. There was one car in the driveway, and the house telephone hung on the kitchen wall.

The three main characters you'll soon meet are an amalgam of six buddies and me. They are blended into Frank, Chase, and Griff; best friends from their Bon Air Village neighborhood—*my* neighborhood. These fictional boys will, hopefully, win your admiration for their resourcefulness, and your respect for their upstanding character.

For the reader, I desire to encourage values that are rooted in kindness, truth, loyalty, forgiveness, and a spirit of adventure in every day!

My thanks in this endeavor go to my wife, Debbie; to our sons Andrew and Jonathan, and to their wives Christina and Emily. They all encouraged me and assisted in refining this book into what you are seeing. Our grandchildren Grant, Iris, and Ellie, inspire me in their own ways daily. Melinda continues to be a terrific sounding board, and even though she would deny the credentials of an editor, she is every bit that.

Thank you to the young men pictured on each book cover: James, Davis, and Jonah. You guys are the best!

Greg Golden

About The Author

Greg Golden grew up in middle America, the youngest of three children and the only son of a pastor. Greg's love for literature was first demonstrated when at the age of ten he ran out of the forty-three Hardy Boys books available to read, and he wrote one for himself.

After college, his career path took him to Mobile, Alabama, where he met and married Debbie. There they raised two sons, and those sons and wives have given them numerous grandchildren--the newest loves and diversions in their lives.

Greg is an ordained minister, and he frequently mentors those who come across his path seeking encouragement and guidance.

Contents

Frank handed the small wooden box to Chase. Chase lifted it above his head and turned around on the ladder to put the box where it was before it fell. As he was about to set it down, he noticed faint writing on the bottom. "Hey, I hadn't seen this before! Donnie, did you notice these words?"

"No! No, I didn't! Hand it here for a second. Let's take a look." Donnie reached up and took the box from Chase, then carried it into the center of the room under the light of a table lamp. The three friends leaned in from behind Donnie to examine the faded but mostly readable message. The handwritten script letters were ornate with long loops and serifs added to the words.

Chase almost shouted. "Oh, man! What in the world did we find? What is this about, anyway?"

From "Password To Meade Manor"

Password To Meade Manor

HIDDEN IN PLAIN SIGHT

CHAPTER 1

"Can you bring the boat any closer?" Chase lifted a lopsided plastic litter bag with both hands. "I've got more to add to our collection."

"I'll be there in a second," Frank replied from twenty feet offshore, slowly navigating his father's Jon boat. "I just need to work my way around some of these submerged tree stumps."

The two friends were near the water's edge of a rambling, pre-Civil War estate on the outskirts of Lewisville. It was nearly 4 o'clock on the third Saturday of September, and they, along with their pal Griff, had been busy supervising a dozen Cub Scouts who were picking up litter along a portion of shoreline by the New Haven River.

As Frank met Chase at the riverbank, Chase added another bag to a half-dozen already collected. Griff stood nearby on the wide, grass levee with his back to the water. He and the den leader kept a watchful eye on the third- and fourth-graders in their blue uniforms. About half of the boys were focused on the cleanup project. The other half wandered around the slope of lawn that extended from the hedgerow down to the bank of the river. The sun had kept the air warm, but lengthening shadows and an occasional cool gust of wind reminded Griff he was glad he wore a jacket. A light haze overhead hinted that someone somewhere upwind was burning leaves. That precise moment on that very day seemed to him a snapshot of how a fall afternoon was supposed to feel, look, and smell.

"Focus, guys!" Griff pleaded with the dozen Webelos and Bears. "This is taking more time than it should!"

Cub Scout Den 11 and its leaders were assigned the job of Waterway Cleanup for their project of the month. It was perfect timing because Lewisville's River Festival was only a week away. On the following Saturday, that same stretch of lawn at the old Meade estate—along with the rest of the shoreline from Driskell Creek to the boat launch—would be full of people. If the festival day turned out like it had in past years, several hundred Jeffers County residents and their lawn chairs and picnic blankets would cover this prime observation spot. It was the absolute best place to view the parade of decorated boats and homemade rafts—each of them competing for the coveted Mayor's Cup trophy.

For the residents of this midwest community of 11,000, the Fall River Festival was a tradition that extended as far back as the end of World War II. The boat parade, the picnicking, the band concert, and the sack races marked the beginning of autumn. From that day going forward, the weather would begin to cool, and the daylight hours would grow noticeably shorter. Except for a possible few days of Indian Summer, sweaters and corduroy pants would begin to replace t-shirts and cutoff shorts.

Griff sighed as he watched three Bears chase a brown and gold butterfly. Farther away, two Webelos wrestled on the thick, fescue grass. *"Come on, guys!* We're not here to play!" he pleaded.

The only boys who seemed to hear Griff were the few compliant rule-followers—the ones who almost always did the right things anyway. The rest of them continued to roll down the hill, have "sword" fights with sticks they'd found, and romp in circles with their pals—unfazed by Griff's protests.

The last two months had been dry across the region, and the water level of the New Haven River at Lewisville was several feet lower than usual. As on most waterways, trash, bottles, and old tires floated downstream and littered the banks. Because of a bend in the river where Driskell Creek emptied into it, little whirlpools formed, and they trapped debris among the cattails and water reeds in the very place where the Scouts were working.

While Griff kept watch over the youngsters, Frank piloted their garbage collection boat. Chase wore hip waders and sloshed back and forth in the shallows of the river transferring the full litter bags from the bank to the Jon boat.

"Ok, this is as close as I can get my boat to you, Chase. If you can work your way over here, I can grab your bag," Frank said. He steered the Jon boat toward his friend, then switched off the electric trolling motor. After a few seconds of coasting in silence, the flat-bottom boat thunked one submerged tree trunk and bounced off another. Finally, the gray aluminum craft held steady between two cypress stumps.

"If everyone brings me what they've collected," Chase began, "I'll probably have half a bag more for you." He pointed into the distance and continued, "And after that, I'll drag those two old tires over there out of the water.

You don't have room for them in your boat, anyway, and we can come back later for them."

Griff Jenkins, Chase Spencer, and Frank Whidden all lived within a few blocks of each other in their Bon Air Village neighborhood. Except for their earliest years, they had known one another as best friends for all of their lives. They began their Cub Scout careers together, much like the boys in their charge on this day. In the coming year, all three friends expected to complete their prerequisites and qualify for the rank of Eagle. The only part of the process that remained was for each boy to appear before their Board of Review. But today, the three buddies volunteered their time because of their love for Scouting. They hoped to be positive role models for the youngsters they were supervising.

"Sounds good, Chase," Frank concurred. "I think I'll have just enough charge in my battery to get back to the boat launch. If you, Mr. Baldwin, and Griff can herd the boys to the van, I'll meet you there. I'll be going against the current, so be patient with me," Frank chuckled. "And if the battery dies, I'll just use my oars."

Over the next few minutes, Chase trudged back and forth among the Cub Scouts. He gathered their collected litter, closed and tied the bag's opening, then stepped back into the water. As he stood among the cattails, he hoisted it onto one shoulder and supported the load with both hands.

"That's 99% of it," Chase declared while placing the bag on the Jon boat. "I can't say that we got every gum wrapper and bottle cap, but things should be cleaned up enough for the festival."

On the hillside, Griff took a headcount of the rolling and falling down youngsters. He put two fingers to his lips and whistled. Griff Jenkins had one of those enviable, piercing whistles that came from the exact placement of fingers to lips. Many times he had tried to teach his power whistle to Chase and Frank, but neither of them could come close to the ear-splitting sound Griff's made.

Once he had the boys' attention, Griff cupped his hands to his mouth and announced, "Let's head for the van, guys. We're finished with our project. Most of you did a good job and can be proud of your work!"

Frank switched the trolling motor into reverse and slowly backed away from the shore and into the river flow. Chase turned away from the boat and sloshed toward land. The last of the Cub Scouts was nearly out of view as the youngsters walked and skipped toward the church van that was idling at the boat launch. Chase was almost out of the water when an object caught his eye. It was the lid from an ice chest, and it was in a place along the bank where he had not been all afternoon—beneath a patch of willows. The Cub Scouts hadn't seen the muddy lid and couldn't have reached it from the shore, anyway. Getting close to it would take Chase a few extra minutes, but it was the largest piece of litter that he'd observed. It would be fitting for this to be the last item collected.

Pushing through the low-hanging willow branches and water reeds, Chase arrived at the lid and leaned toward it. He extended his arm, but with only the tips of two fingers able to touch the lid, it didn't budge.

"That's weird," he said under his breath. He ducked a little lower and stretched his upper body as far as he could.

Something seemed to hold it tightly. He stood upright and with both hands, he spread the reeds far enough apart to make an even wider path for himself, then took a final step forward.

"Huh? What in the world?" he exclaimed under his breath.

Half below water and a half above, concealed by the reeds and flowering rush, were heavy timbers outlining a door into the riverbank! Algae and rust marked where the waterline had been for many years. Except for the recent drought that lowered the level of the river, no one could have possibly seen this rusty door. It would normally have been fully submerged. Chase pushed farther through the willow branches and reached one hand into the murky water. He touched the door where he imagined a knob would be, and in that place he felt a large padlock. It was looped through a hasp that seemed to be coated with rust and sediment.

....

At the boat ramp, Mr. Baldwin backed the church van and the boat trailer far enough into the river so that Griff and Frank were able to winch the Jon boat securely in place. They threw a tarp over the collection of litter bags and tied it all neatly with a length of rope.

"I wonder what's keeping Chase?" Frank questioned.

"It *is* kinda hard to walk when you're wearing those waders," Griff surmised. "I'm sure he'll be here soon."

In another moment, the top of Chase's head and then his shoulders appeared bobbing beyond the rise of the gravel road. In no time, Chase stood next to the idling van. He held the foam lid, and he was smiling from ear to ear. "Help me get these waders off, if you would, guys."

With no explanation, continuing to grin, and without saying a word Chase stowed the waders under a seat in the boat.

Griff's curiosity got the best of him. "What's with the smile?"

Leaning close to both of his friends, with a tantalizing whisper Chase announced, "I'll tell you when we get back to the church."

Within five minutes, the troop leader, Mr. Baldwin, navigated the two-lane road into Lewisville and turned into the Faith Family Church parking lot. Parents of the Cub Scouts were assembled there to receive their sons and hear of the adventures of their afternoon project.

"Everyone did good work," Marvin Baldwin announced to the gathering of proud moms and dads. "The Fall River Festival committee appreciates their help, and the boys' work today completes their Community Service Achievement requirement. Thank you for coming out, boys."

"Help me unhook this trailer, guys," Chase directed. The three gathered around the hitch and cranked the front support wheel down. They then released the ball lock and lifted the tongue of the trailer and rolled it away from the van.

"So, what was it that was so funny—or whatever you were

trying *not* to say back at the boat launch?" Griff asked.

"After you left me, Frank—and while you were rounding up the boys, Griff—I noticed another big piece of litter."

"That foam thing you were carrying?" Griff asked.

"Right! It was wedged under some willow branches in a part of the bank where I hadn't been. When I got over by it, it was stuck on something, and I couldn't get a good grip on the thing without moving in close. When I reached through the reeds to grab it, I saw a door that was partly underwater."

"You mean like a door floating in the water? Something somebody had thrown in the river?" Frank asked.

"*No!* I mean an old, iron door that was attached to a frame. The door was upright like it led into the side of the riverbank!"

"*You're kidding*, right?" Griff asked excitedly. "That makes no sense! What in the world would a door be there be for?"

"Yeah, where would it go?" Frank added.

"We're gonna find out!" Chase replied confidently. "I've never been in that exact part of the river before—by the Meade place—but we need to find a reason to go back and explore some more."

"Well, it's too dark for that now. Tomorrow is Sunday, so I guess it'll have to be next weekend," Griff answered.

"Yeah," Chase added. "You know how I love a good mystery, and this one is looking outstanding!"

....

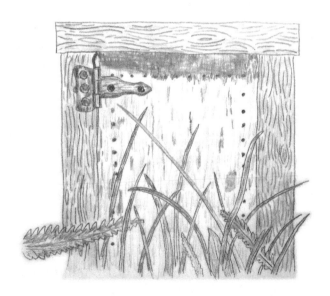

THE ASSIGNMENT

CHAPTER 2

The Monday morning tardy bell at Lewisville Middle School finished ringing. The lively chatter of conversations in Mrs. Crawford's homeroom settled into a soft murmur. The three boys were barely seated at their desks when the loudspeaker above the chalkboard beeped a warning that the morning prayer, Pledge of Allegiance, and announcements were about to begin. Following several amplified clicks, Mr. Barnes, the school's vice-principal, blew two times into the microphone. It was his usual way of getting the attention of the 319 students in the dozen classrooms.

"Good morning, students. I hope everyone had a nice weekend. There are a few things that I need each of you to take note of, so listen closely."

Most everyone stopped stirring at their desks and gave him their full attention.

Eugene Barnes continued. *"This Friday, the cafeteria will be closed so we can get ready for our part of the town's Fall River Festival. On that day, we won't be serving our usual delicious meals, and you'll need to bring a sack lunch from home."*

Upon hearing his description of the cafeteria food, several of the other boys exchanged eye-rolls and grins. One of them acted out the motions of suddenly becoming ill.

However, Mrs. Crawford quickly restored order with a loud rap across the desk with her ever-present wooden ruler.

"I need the following people to report to the school office at 2:30: Nancy Gordon, Ellen Cosgrove, Griff Jenkins, Frank Whidden, Beth Hutchins, and Chase Spencer. Would the six of you please come at the end of the day for your assignments?"

The other announcements faded into the background. They were the usual checklist of things like "Don't forget to pay the deposit on your yearbook orders," and "Remember to support the school's football game on Thursday night."

Chase turned around to face Frank who was seated across the aisle and two seats back. He quietly mouthed the words, *"What assignment is he talking about?"*

Frank shrugged and raised his eyebrows, silently saying, *"I have no idea!"*

....

During the breaks between the class periods and while they ate lunch in the cafeteria, the three friends ventured humorous guesses along with their concerns about the meeting with Mr. Barnes. The girls—the other three members of the group—seemed less troubled. But for the Bon Air boys, the final class period of the day couldn't wrap up soon enough.

The dismissal bell rang through the empty corridors of Lewisville Middle School. Before its sound faded, classroom doors everywhere flew open, and the hallways filled with students. Frank, Griff, and Chase joined the moving sea of people, each of whom was headed for his or her locker to pack up and leave. The three friends gathered their jackets and backpacks and met next to the water fountain.

"This should be interesting," Chase speculated as they strolled toward the office. "Everyone that Mr. Barnes named is in our grade, but I can't think of anything that the six of us have in common."

"I guess we'll know in a few minutes," Griff surmised.

The three girls joined the boys in front of the school office, and they entered the room together.

"Mr. Barnes is waiting for you, students. Follow me." Their guide was Evelyn Wyatt, a slender woman wearing a navy blue skirt and white, puff-sleeved blouse. As she spun sharply on her heel to lead them, the boys noticed a bright yellow pencil stabbed through the bun of her mostly-gray hair. The sight of the suspended pencil caused each boy to chuckle under his breath. Within a dozen steps, the six middle schoolers passed through a half-door that was held in place by spring-loaded hinges—the kind that let it swing freely in both directions. They all stopped at the vice-principal's door and waited for Mrs. Wyatt to signal the okay to proceed into his office.

"Come in, come in," said a smiling Eugene Barnes. "Come on in, close the door, and have a seat."

Mrs. Wyatt let the students enter, and then she pulled the door shut, leaving them alone with the vice-principal.

"I imagine you are wondering why I called your names this morning. First, let me say that no one is in trouble." Hearing those words, the students visibly relaxed and exhaled in unison.

Mr. Barnes paused and smiled. "The six of you are here because of your excellent work. Your history teacher, Mr. Stevenson, shared the rough drafts of your research papers with me. All of you have written fine material on different aspects of the War Between the States. As it happens, this Saturday, Lewisville has the distinct honor of hosting a special guest. He is the descendant of a general in the Union Army, and he is returning to speak to the members of our town's Historical Society. His name is Colonel Atchison Meade, and he is an instructor at our nation's War College. The colonel is in his seventies, but as a boy, he made his home in Lewisville. He hasn't lived here in over fifty years, but he grew up at his family's place by the river. I'm sure some of you have passed Meade Manor out on the edge of town."

Mr. Barnes continued. "The reason I've asked you here is because I have arranged for you to spend some time with him on Saturday morning at his family's home. You can ask him any questions about his relative, General Charles Meade. The troops under the General's command fought in some of the most important Civil War battles of our state. I thought you would enjoy hearing from him because he learned about those engagements directly from his great-grandfather. After the boat parade, he'll be speaking to the Historical Society, but he has reserved the hour before it begins to have time with you students."

....

The bicycle ride to their neighborhood was less than a mile, and the crisp, late September air felt refreshing to the three friends after being indoors all day.

"I don't know how you guys feel, but I'm excited about meeting Colonel Meade," Frank said. "To be related to a famous war hero, boy—that has to be really special!"

"I've wanted a reason to go inside that house for a long time! This is perfect, and it'll be good to hear about the things he has done while in the military!" Griff added.

"I don't know when we'll be able to do it, but I still want to get back to that old door that I found on Saturday. Maybe we can check it out while we're there on the property," Chase offered.

"For sure!" Frank agreed excitedly. "The only problem I see, though, is that on Saturday when we finish meeting with Colonel Meade, people will be all over the lawn with their blankets and chairs. I don't think we can do it then without drawing a lot of attention. But we can try!"

A familiar, deep-blue, customized coupe turned onto Stafford Avenue from Meadow Road. The car approached the three boys, then slowed in the opposing lane. Its driver was Chase's college-aged cousin Donnie. The car rolled to a stop and idled along the curb, its glass-pack mufflers rumbling their deep tone. The boys carefully crossed the avenue and eased up to the driver's open window.

"Hey, Donnie," Chase said. "Are you on your afternoon route?"

Donnie delivered the morning and afternoon editions

of the Lewisville Ledger on the south and east sides of town. Chase, Griff, and Frank respected him as a positive example and role model. Donnie had helped them solve past mysteries.

In the opinions of the three friends, he had the coolest car in the county. He had personally customized the coupe adding white tuck-and-roll leather to the seats, and a flawless, metallic paint job. Curiously, the car's two front doors had no handles. Donnie removed them and covered the holes so perfectly that a person couldn't tell that door handles ever existed there. Somehow, he was able to open either front door from the outside without touching his car. No matter how closely the boys watched, they could never figure out his secret. Each time they pleaded for an explanation, Donnie would just smile.

"Yes, and I'm glad that I ran into you three. I was asked to help do some clean-up and painting at the Meade place. When I was there last week delivering Miss Lillian's newspaper, she told me that her younger brother was coming back to town on Saturday. She said she wanted to freshen the paint in a couple of the rooms. The place is pretty gloomy inside. There are some huge pieces of furniture and..."

"You need some big, husky guys to help you move those things, right?" Griff teased.

Donnie laughed. "You guessed it! I'll start painting there Tuesday evening. Could you guys stop by tomorrow around 6:30 and help me pull some of the furniture away from the walls? I'll paint until late that night and again Wednesday night. Then, hopefully, you can come back on Thursday after supper. By that point, I'd need your help putting things back in their places. That would be a huge blessing, and I'd be glad to pay you!"

"Gosh, Donnie, there's no way you could pay us! For all the times you've helped *us*, we'd be *glad* to help you—wouldn't we fellas?" Chase asked. The others nodded in agreement. "Of course!" they both replied.

"Thanks! I need to go get the rest of my route delivered, but I'll look for you tomorrow night!" With a wave of his hand and the screech of white-lettered tires on the pavement, Donnie was soon out of sight.

....

"Breaker, breaker! Are you guys on yet?" The caller on his two-way radio was Frank. It was precisely 8 o'clock, the time on most evenings when the Bon Air boys checked in with each other from their bedrooms using walkie-talkies.

"I'm here!" Chase said.

"You got me!" Griff responded, sounding very much out of breath.

"Did we catch you at a bad time, Griff?" Frank asked jokingly. "You must have been out jogging."

"Not jogging—*push-ups!*" he panted into his two-way radio. "I gotta keep in shape. You guys remember, I hope, that we have a camping trip leading the Cub Scouts with full backpacks in less than two weeks!"

"Wow! You're right," Chase agreed. "I need to put that on my calendar!"

"Yep, the campsite is up on Wildcat Mountain, or at least partway up," Frank reminded the others, and then his tone of voice changed. "Hey, I have a problem with helping Donnie tomorrow night. My parents told me at supper that our family needs to drive over to Simpsonville for a memorial service. It's tomorrow at 3 o'clock. My mom's great-aunt passed away, and they scheduled her service then. I'll need to get an early dismissal from school. Tell Donnie that I'm sorry and that I'll try to make it up to him. But I definitely can be there to help put the furniture back on Thursday."

"Wow, I am sorry to know about your great-aunt. Please tell your folks that my family and I will be praying for them. And don't worry about needing to be gone," Chase replied reassuringly. "With "Atlas" Jenkins and his push-up muscles, I'm not even sure that *I'm* needed, but I'll tell Donnie what you said."

"Hardy-har-har," Griff interjected with his playful sarcasm. "All the girls like strong boys, so you two can keep on being jealous if you want. It doesn't bother me one bit."

"All right, and be thinking how we're going to get back to the riverbank and that door. The water in the river is only going to keep getting colder every week, and I only have that one pair of waders," Chase explained.

"I've been thinking about what you saw, and I have a theory. You guys realize, don't you, that the water level of the river wasn't always that high along Lewisville?" Frank asked. "They built the dam and those locks a few miles downstream before the turn of the century. The dam was supposed to slow the current in the river, and all of that is what caused the water level to rise along the shore."

"I hadn't thought about that, but yeah, the locks and the dam let the boats and barges pass through safely in the place where there used to be some rough water," Griff added. "Good thinking, Frank!"

Chase agreed. "So it's logical to think the door wasn't underwater at all when someone built it into the levee. It was probably there for lots of years before the locks and dam were added. That makes this whole thing *even more* mysterious. It was pretty obvious to me when I touched and pulled on it that it's locked, and who knows for how long!"

"Well, after we get past this weekend, we should try to figure out what's behind the door! You guys have a good night, and I'll see you in homeroom," Frank said. "Over and out!"

....

FIRST CLUES REVEALED

CHAPTER 3

Just after six o'clock on Tuesday evening, as Chase and Griff headed out on foot to help Donnie, the western sky was ablaze in orange and pink. A strong north wind brought high cirrus clouds into the area, and the wind whistled as it swayed the tops of the trees that lined Wellington Avenue. Their route took the boys directly into the chilly air. Griff wrapped his arms around his chest for added warmth. Neither of them spoke as their sneakers crunched the carpet of brown, red, and yellow leaves that covered much of the sidewalk. When they turned the corner onto Proctor Avenue, they were met with a miniature cyclone of swirling maple and elm leaves. Some of them pressed against the fronts of their jeans for a few seconds, then fell to the pavement again.

"I should've worn a jacket," Chase sighed. "This sweater isn't helping at all."

"It's not much farther," Griff offered, "and hopefully we can help Donnie quickly and get on back home."

Griff continued, "Do you remember the time we dared each other to trick-or-treat at the Meade house? We were probably eight or nine years old back then. It looked so spooky that night, I wasn't sure we would go through with it!"

"Oh, yeah. Who could forget! Frank was the one with the

bright idea. We stood at that gate by the road trying to get our nerve up. I remember thinking about Hansel and Gretel when they went into the woods—how they knocked on the door of the witch's place, not knowing if they'd come out of the house alive! That's about how I felt." Chase smiled to himself.

"Yeah, and I remember when the lady opened her door. She seemed so nice and was surprised that anyone had enough nerve to come up to the porch for Halloween candy," Griff said.

"And because she wasn't expecting anyone, she didn't have any treats to give. But she went and found some cookies for us in her pantry. That was a great night!" Chase remarked.

"Well, here we are, and here's that gate," Griff said. "Let's go in and help Donnie!"

....

On that October 31st night years earlier, the sidewalk had seemed to them as long as a football field. In reality, it was no more than seventy-five feet. It followed a straight line from the gate by the road to the covered porch of the two-story house. Tree roots in random places had cracked and lifted parts of the stone walkway. That damage made it treacherous to walk on in darkness.

Ahead of them, two columns outlined the front door. Light from inside the house shone through the windows of the downstairs rooms, and a lamp lit one of the windows on the second floor. When the boys were nearly at the porch steps, the door opened, and a beam of light illuminated their faces. A silhouette of Donnie stood in the entrance.

"I thought you guys might be getting close. Thanks for helping! Where is Frank? Couldn't he come?"

"His family needed to go out of town this afternoon, so he left school early. He wanted us to tell you he was sorry he couldn't make it," Chase explained, "but he promised to help on Thursday."

"Oh, okay. I think we can do this with just the three of us. Come on in." He turned around to lead them. "Miss Lillian has already gone upstairs for the night. You can pretty easily see what we need to do. It looks to me like some of the furniture hasn't been moved in a hundred years!" Donnie chuckled.

The foyer of the house was narrow and long, and its most prominent feature was a stairway that extended upward along one of the walls. After several steps, it turned at a landing, and then turned again as it rose to the second floor and out of view.

"I'm starting the painting in here," Donnie explained as he gestured toward a room to the left. Chase and Griff followed him into a spacious, formal parlor. Donnie had already set up a ladder and laid out some rollers and brushes. Across several chairs and a love seat, he had stretched drop cloths to protect them from paint spills. "You can see that I couldn't move any of this stuff by myself."

"Everything in here looks *really* heavy!" Griff exclaimed. "No way could you do this alone. I'm glad you asked us."

"What's first?" Chase inquired.

"Those two bookshelf units are going to take some time to unload. I don't think there's a chance that we can slide them away from the walls until we remove the books. I thought we could stack them on the sofas, the table, and the floor in the middle of the room. They can stay there until Thursday."

For the next thirty minutes, the three of them transferred hundreds of books from two sets of shelves onto the furniture and floor. To reach the upper rows, Donnie climbed his ladder, and he handed the dusty volumes to Chase and Griff.

"Man, I would *love* to have the time to look through some of these," Griff observed. "I'll bet there's some great stuff here. You can tell by the covers that these are very old!"

Chase opened a small, tan book with a fragile, leather binding. "Look at this! There's some handwriting and a note inside this one. This date right here says January 26, *1792*!"

"That's very cool, guys, and I'd like to look at them, too, but there's more we need to do. I'll be here painting a long time after you two leave."

"Sorry, Donnie," Griff responded. "I think we've taken enough books away so that we can slide the shelves now."

Donnie agreed. "If the three of us can get on the sides and pull it away from the wall just a little, I can get behind it. From there, I can push while you two guide it another couple of feet. That should be far enough for the painting

I need to do."

With all of their might, they gripped the first of the two eight-foot-tall shelves. They tugged it an inch at a time toward the center of the parlor. "One...two...three, *pull!* One...two...three, *pull!*"

None of them noticed that a plank in the floor directly in front of the bookshelf was warped upward in the middle. On the next pull, the plank snagged the bottom of the shelf, and the wooden case leaned dangerously toward Donnie and the boys!

"Watch out!! It's tipping over!!" Donnie shouted.

"Push back on it—HARD!" Griff yelled.

"We gotta keep it from falling. Push with all your might!" Chase commanded. Adrenaline raced into every muscle in each of them. The shelf wobbled, leaned even more, and with a final heave, they wrestled it backward. It slammed the wall and came to a stop.

"Look out!" Donnie warned as a flat, wooden box slid from behind the trim piece at the top of the shelves. The box and lid flew forward, barely missing Griff's head, and then it crashed onto the floor behind them!

With the shelf now standing safely upright again, the boys and Donnie froze. No one spoke for several seconds as they replayed in the minds what had almost happened. Despite the chilly night and the unheated room, all of them had sweat on their brows—the results of the fifteen seconds of panic they had just experienced.

"We all need to thank the Lord that nobody got hurt," Donnie exclaimed. "I saw my twenty years of life flash before my eyes!"

Chase and Griff managed smiles as they reacted to Donnie. "I was right there with you, buddy!" Griff said.

"What was the thing that fell?" Chase asked.

Donnie turned around and pointed to the carpet. "Gosh, look! Look at that mess!"

On the antique rug in the center of the room between the bookshelf and the sofas was a small wood box—more like a tray with a removable lid. Scattered around it in all directions were scores of discs, each of them a little larger than a nickel.

The three friends got on their knees, and each of them picked up one of the discs to examine it. Donnie scooped up several more and placed them a handful at a time back into the tray. The other boys did the same. They crawled around through half of the room, gathering the wooden pieces that slid and rolled to distant resting places.

"These are really unusual," Griff stated, using his pocket penlight to examine several of the pieces better. "They all have symbols or shapes on them," he said, pointing out the crudely-etched words and drawings.

"Yeah," Chase agreed. "Some of them are painted, and these right here have names scratched into the wood." Holding up two of them, he continued, "And both of these have drawings that look alike. All of them have little holes in the middle."

"I have absolutely no idea what these things are," Donnie stated. "I'll ask Miss Lillian about them when I see her tomorrow. Maybe she knows. In the meantime, guys, unfortunately, we have more furniture to move! Are you still good to stay and help?"

"Sure!" Chase responded. "And I think we learned a lesson with the bookshelves. Next time: look up and around—and *down*, too! Let's get this one pulled out again, and be more careful this time."

. . . .

Frank was already in homeroom at his desk when Chase and Griff arrived and took their seats.

"How'd it go last night—with Donnie?"

"You missed it, buddy! And let me just say," Griff began, "if you see me moving slower than usual in gym class today, I have a very good reason." He stretched his back from side-to-side, groaned, then eased into his desk.

"What Griff is saying, Frank, is he found out while helping Donnie that a few pushups do not Superman make!" Chase chided. "There were a couple of tons of big furniture that we moved!"

"Frank, that house is a *museum* inside," Griff exclaimed. "There are little statues and shelves with row after row of old books. We saw lots of cool artifacts, bayonets, pistols, and souvenirs from different wars. Donnie told us that the Meade men served in both of the World Wars *and* in Korea, too."

"Probably the strangest thing we turned up was a dusty box full of wooden discs with scratchings and little painted figures and names on them," Chase marvelled. "I'll bet there were a hundred discs. Donnie is going to ask Miss Lillian if she knows what they are for."

"Yeah, they were all stored up on top of a huge bookcase where you couldn't see them," Griff explained. "The box fell off when we almost tipped the whole thing over."

"Man, I can hardly wait to go there with you guys Thursday night!" Frank exclaimed. "It sounds like a neat place! The last time I was there, we were just silly kids at Halloween. This time I will definitely appreciate it."

"Yeah, if that house could talk, I'm sure it'd have a lot to say," Griff offered. "Since we have American History for first period, let's try to get there a few minutes early and see if Mr. Stevenson knows anything about Meade Manor."

HISTORY LESSONS

CHAPTER 4

Mrs. Crawford allowed the boys to leave homeroom early to speak with their history teacher.

"No, I'm afraid I don't," Ernest Stevenson explained. "I didn't grow up here, and I've never been inside the house, either. The person I would think might know is Leonard Rigsby. He spoke at a meeting of the Historical Society once, and he seemed to be familiar with several of the older homes and buildings around the county. Do any of you know him?"

Frank's face brightened. "I sure do. *All* of us do. We'll check with him, Mr. Stevenson! Thank you for mentioning Mr. Rigsby."

....

The final bell that announced the end of 6th period couldn't arrive soon enough for the three friends. It had been hard for any of them to concentrate on their classes. Their minds were full of questions about Meade Manor.

"I'm kinda surprised we didn't think of asking Mr. Rigsby ourselves," Griff admitted as they walked through the exit doors and headed toward the bicycle rack.

"Yeah, Frank," Chase said. "He's practically a member of your family. Do you think we could just kinda show up at his house today without calling ahead?"

"I don't see why not. I mean, we pass his place on the way home, anyway. Let's try it. If we see him, I'm sure he won't mind us dropping in."

....

Leonard Rigsby, a widower in his eighties, was one of Lewisville's most respected and beloved citizens. Frank's parents had known him for most of their lives, and he was more like a third grandfather to Frank's dad than merely a neighbor of theirs. His residence was different from almost every other house in Bon Air Village. It was much older—probably from the turn of the century. It was large, with three floors of rooms, and it had four white columns across the front. A broad and inviting porch covered the full width of the house.

Frank and his sister Kate took every opportunity to help the gentleman. Frank was the first person Mr. Rigsby called when he needed his yard mowed or required assistance with a chore around his big house. Kate, a student at the junior college, often drove him to the market or to doctor's appointments.

"He's there! I see him at his mailbox!" Frank confirmed from the lead bicycle as he glanced over his shoulder toward Chase and Griff. The stooped man held his walking cane in one hand and a handful of envelopes in the other.

"Hi, Mr. Rigsby!" Frank shouted as the three boys slowed and walked their bikes across Goldstone Lane.

"Well, hello, Frank. Hello, boys!" the smiling man replied.

"Is school already out?" he asked. "Time gets away from me these days." He chuckled to himself, put several pieces of mail under his arm, and lowered his cane to the sidewalk. "Do you fellows have time for some fresh pie? I made a pumpkin pie this morning, and if you'd care for a slice, I can serve it to you topped off with a dab of whipped cream!"

Griff quickly spoke up. "You don't need to say another word, Mr. Rigsby. We have plenty of time, and we'd *love* some!"

The three boys walked their bicycles up the front yard hill and laid them over in the grass. Frank hurried back to the sidewalk to support the arm of his elderly friend as he climbed the front porch stairs.

"I'm delighted to have your company," Mr. Rigsby acknowledged as he reached the last step. He shuffled across the porch and through the front door. "This big house seems more empty and more lonely with each year. Just make yourselves comfortable at the table in the kitchen. I'll get those slices of pie ready."

"Can we do anything to help?" Chase asked.

"Well, if you could fill glasses for everyone with water from the icebox, that would be splendid!"

"I'll get the forks and napkins," Frank added.

"So how was school today? I hope everyone is making all A's in your courses," he inquired with a wink before turning back to the pie.

"The semester is going well, Mr. Rigsby," Frank replied. All of us are keeping up with our studies. We learned on Monday that we're going to have some time this Saturday before the River Festival with Colonel Atchison Meade. He's coming to town to speak to the Historical Society. The three of us wrote compositions in our history class about the War Between the States, and the vice-principal heard about them. He called us into his office and told us he had worked it out for us to meet with the colonel and ask some questions."

"That is wonderful, Frank! I am proud of each of you boys." Leonard Rigsby carried one plate at a time from the countertop to the table where the boys were seated. Each held a generous serving of pumpkin pie. As he shuffled back to the table for the fourth time, he brought the final plate and sat down. A wistful expression and a slight smile crossed his face. "So old Atch' is coming back to Lewisville. He's hardly been here any that I can think of since he left to attend West Point, and that was more than fifty years ago."

"We wondered if you might know the colonel," Frank remarked. "We're all pretty excited to meet him."

"I guess I was about ten years old when he was born. Yes, I knew his family very well. His only sister, Lillian, is close to my age. She still lives on the family property. A long time ago, I was a little bit sweet on her. I used to carry her books to and from school. It was just a silly thing, of course, but I knew all of the Meades well and spent a great deal of time at Meade Manor back then. The plantation used to take up *much* more acreage then, compared to now."

He paused and looked at the boys. "You're not eating your pie! Is something wrong?"

"Well, actually," Chase began, "we were hoping for that whipped cream you mentioned."

Everyone laughed. "Keep your seat, Mr. Rigsby," Frank suggested, "I can get it from the fridge."

Once each person had eaten his pie and pushed his plate away, Griff asked the question they all had on their minds. "Mr. Rigsby, what can you tell us about the Meade place— well, mostly about the property? Chase and I were there last night. We were helping Donnie move some of the furniture so that he could begin to paint in one of the downstairs rooms. We had some questions and saw a few things that we thought you could help us with."

The kindly gentleman leaned back in his chair, crossed his arms, and began to explain. "It's not the oldest house in Lewisville, but it's most certainly *one* of the oldest, and it has a great history. It was built in the early 1800s. Meade Manor was a full-fledged working plantation with tobacco, cotton, and wheat crops, along with dairy cattle. A few famous racehorses even came from their stables. You boys know, I'm sure, that our state was a border state. I imagine you've studied what that means. There were some people here who owned slaves and others who were totally against slavery. The government here didn't officially align with the Union or Confederate armies. People from all parts around here served in both of those opposing forces."

He continued. "Before the conflicts over slavery began, Samuel and Eleanor Meade had a change of heart and began to feel strongly that no person should be the property of another person. They freed all of their slaves. A few of those freed slaves left this area and headed north to Ohio, Pennsylvania, and even Canada. But surprisingly, most of them chose to stay and work. The Meades said they would treat those who stayed like members of the family, and that's just what they did."

"Shortly before the War Between The States, Samuel and Eleanor died, and Charles, their only son, inherited Meade Manor. He was raised to be a real patriot. He joined the Union army, rose through the ranks, and eventually commanded a battalion of men. His troops were involved in several important battles around our state. While he was away serving his country, his young wife turned Meade Manor into a field hospital. Union troops set up tents and camped on the back acreage. I would imagine that hundreds of soldiers were treated in and around that house. Many of them recovered, but some of them died in those rooms."

"That is amazing, Mr. Rigsby. We had no idea it had such an important part in our history," Griff confessed.

"There's one more thing we were curious about," Chase began. "We found a wooden box..."

The chimes of the doorbell interrupted Chase. A puzzled expression and then a concerned look flashed across Leonard Rigsby's face.

"*Oh, my!* I almost forgot. I have an appointment!" He glanced at a clock on the wall. "That must be Kate! She is driving me to see my doctor. Boys, I never wish to leave good company, and you three are always welcome company. Would you please come back again soon and visit me? I hate to go, but I must leave now."

....

The boys mounted their bikes and entered Goldstone Lane to make their way to Griff's home. "I had no idea the Meade place was so important!" Frank exclaimed. "I sure wanted to be able to ask Mr. Rigsby about those wooden things you guys found."

"Me, too," Chase agreed. "And thinking about Meade Manor, it's funny how you see places all of your life, but don't pay much attention to them after a while."

"All of this talk about history got me to wondering last night," Griff began, "so I pulled out our encyclopedias when I got home. The rock fences along the roads outside of town and all around the county—probably every one of them was built by slaves. If you look closely, there's no mortar holding the stones together, either! The wall that goes around a lot of the Meade place is, I'd bet, a half-mile long if you stretched it out straight. Those men did amazing work! The walls are all made with limestone that came from the rock quarries out by Taylorsville."

"I had no idea!" Frank marveled. "That's just one more example of stuff that's right in front of you every day, but you hardly notice."

The three boys reached Griff's driveway, and they all came to a stop. "I'll talk to you guys on our walkie-talkies later," Griff said. "Be thinking of some good questions to ask Colonel Meade. Saturday will be here before you know it."

The others agreed and offered their farewells as they parted to go separate ways.

....

The chimes of the hall clock outside of Chase's bedroom were still ringing the eight-o'clock hour as he switched on his two-way radio to connect with his pals. "Breaker, breaker. Anybody around tonight?"

"I'm here!" Griff announced.

They both waited in the quiet for Frank to enter the conversation. After a half-minute of radio silence, Chase began. "I guess Frank got busy. Griff, was there some homework that I was supposed to do that I missed writing down?"

"I don't think so—at least I hope there wasn't. Maybe that's not what has Frank tied up. He'll probably be along soon."

Before Chase could respond to Griff, they both heard a radio signal break the silence. "I'm here, guys, and if I sound like I'm on the move, it's because I'm walking. My dad needed to take Mr. Rigsby the prescription his doctor wrote for him. Kate was tied up, so I rode along in the car. I grabbed my radio when we left. Dad went home, and I stayed to visit. I planned to ask more about Meade Manor."

A hiss and some static came through the walkie-talkie receivers. Frank knew how much the others were anticipating that information, and he was intentionally playing with their curiosity.

"*Well?*" Griff asked eagerly, "are you going to leave us hanging or tell us what you found out?"

As Frank walked in the cold evening, the wind whooshed across his walkie-talkie microphone and into the others' radios. "I told him Chase had seen the metal door into the levee, and I just *barely* mentioned the discs. But I'm afraid I mostly struck out again. Someone called him long distance after my dad had been gone for only a minute or two. I waited for about fifteen more minutes while he was on the telephone, then I finally waved goodbye and let myself out the front door."

....

A CRYPTIC MESSAGE

CHAPTER 5

Griff caught up with Frank in the hallway of Lewisville Middle School. His friend was dialing in his locker combination numbers. "You didn't help me sleep any better last night with what you told us," Griff admitted.

"I know. I couldn't stop thinking about how close we are, but what we still don't know." Frank slipped off his backpack, stowed it with his jacket, then closed the locker door. "It's like we almost get some answers, but then something happens and interrupts us."

Chase arrived at that moment and stepped up to his locker, a couple of yards away from theirs. "Frank, are you talking about your visit with Mr. Rigsby last night?"

"Yeah, I'm afraid so," he replied.

"Well, at least tonight we can find out if Donnie learned anything new from Miss Lillian," Griff offered. "You two are still planning on helping to move the furniture after supper, aren't you?" They both nodded.

The 7:55 warning bell echoed through the hallway and ended their conversation. The three of them made their way into their homeroom class and took their seats. A few minutes later, the voice of Mr. Barnes droned over the loudspeaker. With the boys' added anticipation of finishing their classes and meeting up with Donnie, the rest of the day seemed twice as long as usual.

....

"It's got to be at least twenty degrees warmer now than when school started!" Griff commented as the three friends pushed open the school door and stepped into the afternoon sunshine.

Chase slipped his sweater over his head, shoved it into his backpack, then mounted his bicycle. "I'm going to enjoy this weather, however long it lasts." They pedaled away from the school grounds and onto Meadow Road. "So, what time can you two be free to head over and help Donnie? He called me last night and said he'd be there right after he finished with his afternoon paper route— probably by 6 o'clock."

"You want to come to my house?" Griff asked. "We can ride our bikes—let's say around 5:50?"

"That works for me. Right after we eat, I'll come straight to your place," Chase replied.

"Me, too," Frank said.

....

The evening air of Indian Summer on Thursday night called for short sleeve shirts and jeans. They pedaled the six blocks quickly and coasted through the sidewalk gate. As they entered the property, the boys heard the rumble of the coupe's motor ahead of them. Donnie had just arrived in the driveway that circled in front of the Meade house. Once he turned off his engine, silence gave way to the voices of crickets. Donnie switched off his lights, exited his coupe, and strolled toward the front porch.

"We're here!" Chase hollered. Donnie stopped and turned to see the three friends. After several seconds the boys reached the porch, laid their bikes in the grass, and joined him.

"I sure appreciate you guys coming. I'm mostly finished in the parlor, so getting the furniture back against the walls won't take long."

"Whatever you need us to do, we're ready to pitch in," Frank answered.

The front door was slightly ajar, and Donnie tapped twice, waited, then pushed it open. No one was in sight, so the four of them walked into the foyer. Sounding far away in another part of the house, they heard a man's muffled voice and then a much softer woman's voice.

"We're here, Miss Lillian!" Donnie spoke loudly in the direction of the voices. "We've come back to finish downstairs!" He waited for a response. After several more seconds, they heard footfalls, and soon a small woman in a floor-length housecoat entered the foyer. Following behind her was a slim, black man. They assumed him to be around thirty years old. Miss Lillian had pale skin, and her bright crimson lipstick with dark, drawn-on eyebrows seemed out of place to them considering the time of day. An abundance of pink rouge accented her cheekbones.

"Oh, thannnk you, Donnie, and thannnk you, boys! I am so looking fah-ward to Sat-uh-day, having mah brutha' home ah-gain." Miss Lillian spoke with a drawl that seemed held over from the deep south of generations ago.

"You're welcome, Miss Lillian," Donnie replied. "We'll be here for a few hours. I'll let you know when we finish up and are leaving—that is if you're still awake."

"Oh, dah-ling, that's fine. Cyrus can lock up ever-thang when y'all are red-ah to go."

The tall fellow leaned forward and extended a weathered hand to Donnie. His fingers and arms bore callouses and scratches. It was evident that he was a laborer—someone who had spent time working with his hands. "I am glad to make your acquaintance. I live here on the property," he said, "I'll come around later and close up the house when you're gone."

"It's nice to meet you, Cyrus. I didn't realize anyone besides Miss Lillian lived here."

"Oh, yes, sir. I grew up here. My daddy grew up here, and his daddy and granddaddy all worked here when they were younger."

"All right, then. I'm sure we'll be a couple of hours at least," Donnie stated.

Cyrus acknowledged those words with a quick nod of his head, then both he and Miss Lillian turned, strolled toward the rear of the house, and continued their conversation until their words faded entirely.

Donnie described the job before them as he led the boys into the parlor. "The first order of business is to get these bookshelves moved and then load all of those books back on them—just like they've been for the last hundred years or so." He grinned as he pointed to the sea of books and motioned toward the first of the large bookcases.

For the next half-hour, the four of them worked together. They moved the furniture—lifted and slid short and tall credenzas and cabinets against three of the room's walls. When those tasks were finished, they returned hundreds of books to the shelves of the two cases.

"I didn't mention it yet, but I need to ask another favor. Yesterday Miss Lillian asked me if I could paint in one more room—the colonel's original bedroom when he grew up here. So if you can stay with me a little longer tonight, upstairs there's a bed, an armoire, and a dresser that need to be moved."

"Of course. We can do that!" Griff assured him as the others nodded in agreement.

"It's just to freshen up the paint on the baseboards, chair rails, and door frames," Donnie explained. "I'm not painting the walls."

As the four of them finished filling the bookshelves, Griff spoke. "We've been curious about those discs. Did you, by chance, ask Miss Lillian what she knows about them?"

"I showed her the box yesterday, and she seemed just as confused as we were. She told me she'd never seen them before. And that reminds me—I told her we'd put them back where we found them." He pointed to the top of the largest bookcase.

"I'll get the stepladder and do it now," Chase offered.

The wooden box was on a table in the center of the room. Griff picked it up and carried it to Chase, who had already stepped onto the ladder.

Frank moved quickly to where they were standing. "Before you put them back, let me take a look at one. I haven't gotten to see them yet." He removed the lid and examined several of them. "Yeah, I see what you mean. They are sure unusual. And these little drawings—I'd love to know what they're supposed to mean."

"Maybe the colonel can tell us about them," Griff offered. "That needs to be one of our first questions when we have our chance to speak with him on Saturday."

Frank handed the box up to Chase. Chase lifted it over his head and turned around to return it to where it was stored before it fell. As he was about to set it down, he noticed some faint writing on the bottom of the box. "Hey, I hadn't seen this before! Donnie, did you notice these words?"

"No! No, I didn't. Hand it here for a second. Let's take a look." Donnie took the box from Chase and carried it to the center of the room into the light of a table lamp. He carefully held the lid and the bottom together and turned the box over. The three friends leaned in from behind Donnie to examine the faded, but mostly readable, message written there. The script was ornate with long loops and serifs added to the handwritten words.

Star will lead the longing heart
Earth doth guide the eye
Water proves the promised _____
Word and key disclose

Chase almost shouted. *"Oh, man! What in the world did we find? What is that about, anyway?"*

"I don't believe it's like a *poem* poem," Frank replied. "It seems more like a riddle—a cryptic riddle!"

"I can't quite read the word that's after *promised*," Chase conceded. "It's faded pretty badly."

"Yeah," Griff agreed. "If we can somehow decipher what this riddle, or *whatever* it is, means, it might help us figure out those wooden things in the box! You can believe I'll be thinking long and hard about it!"

"Guys, I asked Miss Lillian for permission, and I showed one of the discs to a professor at my college," Donnie stated. "He didn't know what it was, either, so I guess if we're going to make any sense out of them, it's up to us to do it."

Donnie began to walk toward the ladder next to the bookshelf. "Wait!" Griff said anxiously. "I'd like to write down those words on the bottom of the box and start trying to figure out what they mean. You guys know how much I like trying to break codes!"

"I don't think I've seen any blank paper in the parlor, but I have a note pad and pencil in my car," Donnie reported as he handed the box to Frank. "I'll be right back." He disappeared into the foyer, and they heard the front door open and close behind him.

Frank looked at his friends anxiously. "Guys, we kinda need to move this along and finish pretty soon, especially if Donnie needs help upstairs, too."

"You're right," Chase agreed. "I have a Biology research paper due, and I'm pretty sure you guys do, too."

For the next few minutes, the three boys continued placing the final books on the proper shelves. Soon they heard Donnie crossing the porch and move into the foyer. He slowly entered the parlor holding a tablet and pencil, but a troubled expression covered his face. "What's wrong?" Chase asked.

"It's my wallet," he sighed. "It was on my front seat, and now it's not there. I'm almost positive that I left it there because my window was open, and after I closed the door, I tossed it back into my car. It was full of cash. I had over $170 in it from my paper route collections this afternoon. It's gone—all of it."

"Maybe it's on the floor," Griff suggested.

"Or maybe it fell between the other seat and the door," Chase offered.

"I thought of all that. I got my flashlight from the glove box and checked in the front and in the back seat—under everywhere. It's *not* in my car."

"Who could have taken it?" Frank questioned. "The only people around here besides us are...." He stopped speaking in mid-sentence, and his words faded into silence.

Donnie glanced toward the empty foyer. "I don't want to believe it happened like that."

....

TICKING OF THE CLOCK

CHAPTER 6

"I'll worry about my wallet later," Donnie expressed as he handed the tablet and pencil to Griff. "Write that riddle down, then let's head upstairs. I don't want your parents to be upset with me for keeping you three out late on a school night." Donnie tried to smile, but it was apparent to the boys that he was troubled.

The others waited while Griff jotted down the lines of the riddle. The boys then followed Donnie to the staircase in the entryway. Partway up the steps on the first landing they reached an ornate grandfather clock. Frank stopped to watch its polished brass pendulum swing slowly as it counted the seconds. Griff and Chase paused with Frank. The reddish-brown mahogany clock towered over the three of them.

Donnie continued up the stairs but then turned around when he noticed they had stopped following him. "I don't want to be pushy, guys, but we need to get this done so you three can get home."

"Sorry, Donnie," Chase exclaimed. "but this clock is amazing!"

"Yeah," Griff agreed. "I wonder how old it is."

. . . .

The guest bedroom on the second floor was furnished with king-sized everything. Although not as large as the parlor, the pieces of furniture and the massive bed took another fifteen minutes of their time to move to the center of the room.

Back on the stairway landing, the Westminster chimes of the clock announced the new hour. The four friends paused and silently counted each peal: *Bong, bong, bong, bong, bong.*

"Um, I know *that* can't be right," Chase commented.

Griff looked at his wristwatch. "It's seven o'clock—not five o'clock."

Frank cleared his throat and began to explain. "Pendulum clocks have two sets of weights. The first set operates the clock, and the other one makes the chimes work. If you only want the hands of the clock—the part that tells time—to operate, you would wind just those weights. I bet Miss Lillian forgot and let the chimes wind down. It must have run out as it was ringing the hour. Donnie, do you think it'd be okay if I fixed that for her so the clock can continue to chime?"

"I can't think of any reason why she'd mind—but we'll need to have the key. We're finished here—I mean, *you three* are finished up here. I'll be painting for another couple of hours, but let me walk with you guys back downstairs. We can check about the clock on the way."

When the four of them reached the landing, sure enough, the pendulum was swinging back and forth. However, looking through the glass of the lower clock door, they could see that one of the two weights had reached the bottom of the cabinet. In that position, the chimes wouldn't be able to ring.

Donnie carefully unlatched the clock's lower door and opened it. "I'm guessing that most people would store the wind-up key inside here," he explained.

Chase stepped forward. "I'll feel around on the inside for it." He moved his hand along the edges. "There's nothing in here, at least as far as I can tell."

"Try checking up higher," Frank suggested.

"Got it!" Chase exclaimed. He removed a black, metal key and handed it to Donnie.

"Well, here's a problem. This isn't a clock key," Donnie reported. "This one is the kind of key you'd use for an old lock—and I mean *really* old—like for a jail door or something."

"Like maybe for a *padlock*?" Chase asked.

"Maybe. Keep looking," Donnie encouraged. "Miss Lillian is too short to store the key up very high. It's gotta be hanging on a hook in there somewhere, but I would think it's down lower."

Chase felt along the bottom of the door, and in no time, his fingers touched a small hook holding a second key. "This must be it!" he declared, handing the brass key to Donnie.

"That's the one, all right." He opened the upper door and inserted it in its hole. "See how it fits right here on the face of the clock. I'm going to wind it." Donnie carefully rotated the brass key. "When I turn it, you can see that the weight is coming up. I'll stop when it reaches the seat board or when the key gets too hard to turn. That should make it good to ring the chimes for another seven or eight days."

"What are you going to do with that other key, Donnie?" Griff asked

"Put it back where we found it, I guess," he offered. "Why?"

Chase quickly interrupted Griff. "Um, it's just very cool to see things this old. Let me have one more look at it before we go."

Chase and his friends studied its size and shape. The black key had specks of rust on the surface. Its rough edges suggested that it was hand-forged. Chase gave it back to Donnie, who hung it on a nail inside the lower clock door.

"I appreciate your help, guys—both tonight and on Tuesday," Donnie stressed. He led them down the remaining steps, and they walked together to the front door.

"We're going to pray that you can find your wallet," Frank said. "I'm gonna believe that you will."

"Let me speak a prayer for that," Chase volunteered. *"God, you know all things, and this wallet is important to Donnie. We pray that you would show him where it is and that none of the money would be missing. Amen."*

"Thanks for that, Chase. I'll see you guys soon. Goodnight."

The boys stepped into the damp, evening air. "And tell your parents thanks for letting me borrow you!" The three friends smiled as the door latched behind them.

·······

By 6:30 on Friday morning, Frank was already seated at his kitchen table when his dad walked into the room. In front of Frank were a half-empty cereal bowl, an untouched glass of orange juice, and two encyclopedia volumes. The "W" book was open to the section of *The War Between the States*. The "L" volume was open to an article about *Locks and Dams*.

"Oh, good morning, Dad," Frank said. His eyes never left the "L" book.

"Is this last-minute homework, son? You aren't usually up at this hour unless you're going fishing—and, *wow*, you're even dressed for school!" He smiled and stepped to the counter, where he plugged in the coffee pot. "What are you looking for? Can I help with anything?"

"The guys and I have been helping Donnie while he's painting for Miss Lillian inside the old Meade Manor house. The other night when I couldn't go, Chase and Griff were moving some of the furniture and came across some wooden discs. They were stored on top of a big bookshelf in a box that was covered with dust. We've been trying to figure out what they're for."

Mr. Whidden removed a coffee mug from a cabinet, put it next to the percolator, and sat down across from his son. Frank continued. "There were four or five different drawings scratched into the wood. No one that we've talked to seems to know anything about them."

"I would think that the Lewisville Historical Society members might be your best folks to ask about those items. You might want to check with them."

"We thought Mr. Rigsby would know, but we didn't get to ask him when we went to his house a few days ago. We are planning on asking Colonel Meade when we see him tomorrow morning. If he can't help us, I'll for sure check with the Historical Society people next week."

....

Saturday morning brought a perfect, cloudless day with temperatures ideal for a lightweight jacket. Griff Jenkins awakened to the aroma of frying bacon and fresh biscuits seeping under his door. He rolled onto his side, sat up on the edge of his bed, and rubbed his eyes. A rumbling on the stairs outside of his room seemed to shake the entire house, and it jarred him fully conscious. Two quick raps sounded on his door, the knob turned, and through the opening came Frank and Chase. They both had on Sunday dress pants, polished shoes, and freshly ironed long-sleeved shirts with neckties.

"Do I know you two?" Griff quipped as he combed his fingers through his thick mop of hair. "And why are you so dressed up?"

"The three of us have places to go and people to meet, buddy! And this isn't just *any* Saturday. Did you forget? We're expected at the Meade place in exactly..." Chase pulled back the cuff of his shirtsleeve and checked his wristwatch. "...exactly fifty-seven minutes."

"Your mom called our moms and invited us for breakfast," Frank explained, "and it looks like the food is almost ready. Your mom thought you were already up and getting a shower, so you need to get with it—quick! We'll be downstairs! No pressure or anything!" Frank grinned as he and Chase strolled out the door.

....

The three boys pedaled their bicycles toward the Meade property, and they noticed more traffic than usual on the roads. "I guess a lot of people want to get good spots along the levee to watch the boat parade. I don't blame them." Griff observed. "The best place for lawn chairs will be filled up early."

Chase agreed. "Where we did our scout cleanup project— that's right where the judges for the parade review the boats. I hope we can find a place for ourselves when we finish meeting with Colonel Meade."

As they arrived at the front gate of the old estate, a car at the curb was just then dropping off Nancy, Ellen, and Beth, the other three students who were invited to meet with Colonel Meade.

"Hey, there!" Chase offered as he greeted them. "Are you excited about the morning? Did you come up with some good questions for the colonel?"

The boys walked their bicycles behind the girls as the six of them approached the house. "I have a few on my list," Beth replied. The other girls shrugged and smiled.

"*Our* list keeps getting longer," Frank explained. "We've

been looking forward to this all week!"

The area above the front entrance was draped with red, white, and blue bunting. The colorful streamer added a cheery, patriotic appearance to the old, whitewashed brick home.

As the students climbed the steps and reached the front door, it swung open. A distinguished-looking black gentleman with short-cropped, mostly-gray hair and wearing a tuxedo stood in the doorway. They guessed him to be in his seventies. The Bon Air boys quickly supposed that the greeter was a relative of Cyrus, the young man they met when they were in the house on Thursday. The suit of clothes the gentleman wore appeared to be a couple of sizes larger than his narrow frame.

"Welcome to Meade Manor! You all must be the students from the school. Colonel Meade is expecting you. Please come in!" He bowed from the waist as he took a step backward into the foyer. When he did, he opened the door even wider for them.

Chase offered a quiet "thank you." The students stepped through the entryway, and the gentleman closed the door behind them.

"My name is Lucius Evans, and I will be taking you to meet with the colonel." Once again, he bowed slightly from the waist and then turned in the direction of the parlor. As he walked, he looked over his shoulder and continued speaking. "If there is anything that you need while you are here, it will be my pleasure to serve you."

"Mr. Evans," Griff began, "I believe we met your son on

Thursday night."

"He's my grandson," the gentleman replied with a chuckle and a wink. "He helps Miss Lillian with this place—as do I. His daddy passed when Cyrus was just a baby. I raised him these years since then. He's a good boy, Cyrus is."

Arriving at the doors of the parlor, Mr. Evans tapped on the opening. With a loud, clear voice, he announced, "Colonel Meade, your guests have arrived!"

....

QUESTIONS UNANSWERED

CHAPTER 7

Across the parlor, they saw the head and shoulders of a man seated with his back to them. He faced an inviting hearth that glowed from a small fire. Once the students were announced, an impressive figure stood and turned toward them. He was taller than they had imagined. His thick gray hair was combed straight back. He wore dress blues and a starched white shirt with a perfectly-knotted tie. His spit-shined black shoes reflected the light from the chandelier that was centered in the room.

"Come in, come in!" His voice boomed with a mixture of authority and kindness. "Please join me here and make yourselves comfortable." He pointed to a grouping of four Victorian armchairs and a settee upholstered in deep-red velvet. Griff, Frank, and Chase knew those chairs well since they had stacked hundreds of books on them. He waited for the six to settle in and then sat across from them in a well-worn leather club chair.

"So," Colonel Meade began, "I understand that you folks are the best writers in your school." The students smiled and glanced at each other. "Your vice-principal contacted me and said each of you was interested in the history and battles that took place in this part of our state. He also mentioned that all of you had shown great skill in your essays about the Civil War." He paused and raised an eyebrow inviting one of them to speak.

"Uh, yes, sir," Frank began. "First of all, thank you for letting us come today. We've been looking forward to meeting with you."

"Mr. Barnes said that we should prepare some questions to ask you, so, since we only have an hour, we'd like to begin—if that would be okay," Griff added.

The three girls went first, and their questions centered mostly on Colonel Meade's duty stations after he received his commission as a twenty-year-old. They were interested in the countries to which his assignments had taken him, and the dignitaries he may have met. The colonel held everyone's interest with his keen memory and stories of the European Theater of battles. He had been a major in Normandy and served under several celebrated generals of the Second World War. The students were amazed to learn that his tours of duty had taken him to four different continents.

As his stories came to an end, the room was silent for only a moment when Chase spoke. "Colonel, all of us grew up here in Lewisville, and we have passed your home probably a hundred times. But we never realized the part it played in the Civil War. Can you tell us about that?"

"I'd be glad to do that. This house was built by Edward Meade. His family made a fortune in the shipping industry, and at one time, the property covered over nine hundred acres."

"From the late 1700s through 1812, France and England were at war. Because of this, American ship owners took the opportunity to transport crops and goods that were raised or made here to both France and England and other countries of Europe. Our ships were considered neutral traders, and although many of them were captured, we continued crossing the Atlantic Ocean with cargo. The tariffs generated by those voyages paid for much of the budget of our young nation. When the ships left for Europe with American crops and goods, instead of coming back empty, many ships traveled home by way of Africa. When they returned, they often carried slaves to be sold in America."

He continued. "I am sorry to say that the Meade ships were, for a time, also guilty of this terrible practice. But by the mid-1850s, Edward Meade's only son, my great-grandfather, Charles, had become an abolitionist. I'm sure you know what that word means. He was very much against slavery. And even though this property was in a border state, my ancestors expressed their desire to see all slaves set free before a war was ignited. I hope that answers your question."

One of the girls raised her hand. "Colonel Meade, what was your favorite memory about growing up here?"

Atchison Meade smiled and leaned forward in his chair. "That is an excellent question. When this house was built and the land was planted, it was entirely self-sustaining. By that, I mean this: they had crops of all types to feed the more than one hundred workers and the family in this house. They raised cattle and poultry for meat and eggs — enough for all who lived here with plenty left over to sell. A stream called Driskell Creek runs through the property, and it empties into the New Haven River. At one time, it powered a gristmill where wheat and corn were ground for flour and meal. But one of the favorite parts of the property was—well, let me show you."

He stood and gestured for the others to follow. Colonel Meade walked to a set of windows at the end of the large parlor and pulled on thick, tasseled cords attached to curtains. The curtains slid back and revealed a broad stretch of the yard with a hedgerow in the distance. Beyond the hedge was the sloping grass levee that led to the banks of the New Haven River. It was the levee the Cub Scouts had spent time cleaning the previous Saturday.

"Just over the hedgerow, between there and the river was once a large vineyard. Concord and Catawba grapes grew all along that area." The colonel pointed to the hedges to the left and right nearly as far as they could see through the windows. "When I was a boy, my sister Lillian and I played throughout the grapevine arbors. We would hide from each other, and sometimes we would stay there for hours and eat so many grapes that I was afraid we might actually turn purple—at least that's what our parents told us. The kitchen helpers picked the grapes and made jam from them for our family and the neighbors around us."

Beyond the hedges, they saw people arriving to watch the River Festival boat parade. The seven of them stood silently for a moment and admired the beautiful autumn day. In the distance, on the river, several pleasure boats and runabouts had positioned themselves and dropped their anchors to view the upcoming parade from the far side of the route.

A plume of smoke from one of the boats caught Griff's eye. *"Hey, look! Something's burning!"* He pointed into the distance. Everyone's eyes joined his and focused on a growing billow of black smoke that came from a blue and white pleasure craft! *"It's on fire!!"* Griff cried. "Guys, we need to get out there. Somebody's gotta help them!"

Chase and Griff were already headed to the door as Frank turned to their host. "Colonel Meade, please excuse us," Frank pleaded. "I don't know what we can do, but..."

"Go on, son, *go*! I pray that no harm comes to anyone!"

The three boys were instantly in a footrace toward the bushes that served as a fence along one side of the house. As they ran, each of them scanned the tall hedge in search of a place that might let the boys pass through and onto the levee. When they neared the hedge Griff was ten steps ahead of Chase and Frank. Without slowing any, he yelled over a shoulder to his friends, *"I see an opening!"*

Griff pointed ahead and then changed his route. The others quickly adjusted their steps to follow the path of their friend. Beyond the border of bushes, they heard the sounds of concerned adults and squeals of children. By now, most people had seen on the river what the Bon Air boys noticed from inside the house.

"We're coming through! Sorry! Please move aside!" The young teenagers dashed through a narrow opening of the hedge wall. The stiff branches caught on their clothing and tore into their skin.

To their amazement, none of the crowd of onlookers had made any effort to reach the burning boat. Its outboard motor was now fully engulfed in reddish-orange flames. The two people on the boat had moved away from the stern and were crouched ahead of the windshield near the bow. Other boats in the vicinity were scrambling to raise their anchors and move, but none of them was close enough to offer a life ring or toss a rope to the burning runabout.

By the time Griff reached the riverbank, he had already removed his tie and unbuttoned and flung aside his dress shirt. He paused at the water's edge long enough to pull off his shoes. All three boys were certified as BSA Lifeguards, and were qualified to attempt this difficult task. Without any concern for how cold the river might be, Griff dove into the water. With powerful freestyle strokes, in less two minutes, he was next to the boat. At nearly the same moment, a passenger on one of the other nearby vessels threw a life ring and rope toward the small craft. It fell far short of the boat's bow.

Griff was panting and shivering as he reached the front of the burning runabout. He held onto the bow and spoke to the two occupants—a grandfather and a young boy, he assumed. "You're going to be okay!" he told them. "I'm going to swim over and get the life ring, and then I'll come back to help you. Sir, in just a minute, I need you to hand the boy down to me. I'll get him to shore. Then you need to come over the side. Don't jump, just lower yourself into the river, and I'll have the life ring with the rope attached ready for you."

With the calm and confidence of an adult, Griff took charge of the frightening situation. He swam to the floating ring with its rope attached, looped his arm through it, and side-stroked back to the boat. The back end of the little craft was now an inferno of flames and had slipped mostly underwater.

"What's the boy's name?" Griff asked the man.

"It's Steven."

"Steven, you're going to be okay. I'm going to take you with me, and we're going to go right over there where those people are." He pointed to the shore. "Sir, hand Steven down to me. The life ring is right here, and once I have Steven, I need for you to come over the side—slowly, feet first. Put the ring over your head, and loop your arm and shoulder through it. The people in that boat over there are going to pull you to safety."

Calmly and confidently, Griff insisted. *"Hand him to me now!"* Despite tears and pleas by the boy, the older man held both arms of his grandson and lowered him into the cold water. Griff immediately grabbed him, turned him around, locked one of his arms around the boy's chest, and began to swim toward the shore. He held firmly onto the trembling youngster. As soon as Griff and the child were on their way to the river's edge, the gentleman did exactly as Griff instructed. In only a minute, the people on the second boat pulled the older man to safety.

At the shore, Chase and Frank were already in knee-deep water. As Griff got closer, they waded farther in to wait for their friend. In a few more minutes, young Steven arrived in Griff's arms, and the two friends assisted both of them onto dry ground. Several onlookers came to the riverbank and offered their jackets and picnic blankets for warmth.

Barely ten minutes had passed since the boys first noticed the wisps of smoke from inside the manor house. The crisis was now over.

......

In the moments after the boys ran out of the house, Miss Lillian placed a phone call to the emergency responders. Thankfully, Sheriff Jenkins and one of his deputies were already nearby directing traffic. Lee Jenkins brought his patrol car as close as he could to the Meade property, and in a single action, he turned off the engine and jumped out of his vehicle. He sprinted toward the broad levee packed with people. Scanning the bystanders near the river's edge, he caught a glimpse of a group that was gathered and assisting the boys. Within seconds he was next to them.

"Dad!" a shivering Griff cried out. *"We got them to safety!"*

"Great work, son!" Lee Jenkins pushed through the group and wrapped both arms around his teenage son—a boy who looked very much like a cocoon wearing a red and white checkered picnic blanket. The sheriff patted him on his head full of wet hair, then looked away into the crowd. "Where are the people from the boat?"

"The little boy is right here," Frank replied as he pointed to Steven standing behind Griff and out of view. The lad was bundled from head to toe beneath three layers of oversized jackets. "He's fine," Frank continued, "and his grandfather is on the Weatherby's boat. They pulled him in on a life preserver, and they're taking him over to the boat ramp now."

"I need to get you three out of these wet clothes," Sheriff Jenkins said. He looked around at the familiar faces of a dozen Lewisville residents—the ones who had assisted the boys. "Can a couple of you folks get the little boy back to his grandfather?"

A husband and wife nodded. "We're neighbors of the family. We'll be glad to do it. We'll take Steven to the boat launch and drive him and his grandfather home."

Chase turned toward the water and saw floating pieces of the burned boat. They were drifting toward the marshy reeds of the riverbank, many of them still smoldering. "Man, what a mess!" he said while shaking his head. "That fire—it's such a shame. I guess they didn't have a fire extinguisher or life vests. That was a big mistake!"

The boys gathered their shoes and Griff's torn shirt, and they walked with the Sheriff toward his patrol car.

"Our bikes are still in front of the main house," Griff noted.

"I'll call Miss Lillian and ask her to look after them until you can come back and get them. I'm sure they'll be fine for now. Did you guys already have your time with Colonel Meade before the excitement began?"

"It was good, Sheriff. The girls went first with their questions. He's an interesting man. But then we saw the smoke, and we missed our chance to ask the things we've been wondering about," Frank lamented. "Maybe when we come back for the bikes, we can have more time to talk with him. I sure hope so."

....

FOLLOWING MORE CLUES

CHAPTER 8

Chase dropped into the chair in his bedroom and picked up his walkie-talkie. For the third time in five minutes, he squeezed the transmit button. "Breaker, breaker, are you guys on?" After a half-minute with no response from either of his friends, he switched off the radio, pushed away from his desk, and walked downstairs.

It was 4:15, and his mother was standing at the kitchen sink, rinsing a colander filled with potatoes. Carol Spencer glanced up to see Chase take a seat at the table. She turned off the faucet, set the container on the counter, and dried her hands. "You look bored," she observed with a sympathetic smile.

"I'm more disappointed than I am bored. The guys and I had big plans for today, and it looks like nothing's going to happen now."

"I would call it an *exciting* day. What you three did was a lot more than nothing. There'll be other Saturdays and other River Festivals. Cheer up, son." She paused, and neither of them spoke for a half-minute. "*Hey*, how would you feel about peeling these potatoes for our supper?"

Chase wasn't sure if she was serious or if this was her way to distract him. "Sure," he groaned. "Um, I mean *sure*! I'd be *glad* to. I was hoping you'd ask!" Both of them knew he wasn't sincere, but he broke into a wide grin anyway, and they both laughed.

Carol Spencer mussed her son's sandy brown hair and suggested, "If you'll go to your dad's recliner and get yesterday's newspaper, you can use that to catch the potato peels."

Chase slid his chair back, stood, then walked into the living room. After several minutes he hadn't returned. "Chase, are you coming back?" He didn't reply. His mother stepped away from the stove and entered the living room. There she found Chase seated in his father's recliner deeply engrossed in a book that was open on his lap. "For a minute, I thought I lost you," she confessed.

"Mom, where did this book come from? Is it dad's?"

"I believe it came in the mail on Wednesday or Thursday. You know that your father belongs to the Book-Every-Month Club. He doesn't keep many of them, but he likes ones that feature American History. What did you find that's so interesting?"

Chase held up the book, turned it around, and showed his mother the open pages. "This drawing looks a little bit like Meade Manor. And the chapter right here is titled *The Underground Railroad*. I'm not sure what that means."

Carol Spencer moved closer and sat on the arm of the recliner. "As I remember from my high school classes, the underground railroad was a series of secret places that were called stations. The stations were locations where some very good people helped those that fled slavery. The places were spread around the southern United States, with some even found in the border states and in the north.

A station could be a barn or a cave or possibly someone's attic or their cellar. The slaves heading north would normally follow directions given to them by someone back home. It was safest to travel at night, and one of the main things that helped them find their way was to look for the Big Dipper constellation. If they walked in the direction of its brightest star, called Polaris or the North Star, they could know they were headed in the right direction."

"That is *amazing,* mom! So you're saying it doesn't have anything to do with trains? Just kinda like a lot of people who wanted to help the slaves get their freedom?"

"Yes, that's how I understand it."

"I had no idea!" Chase exclaimed. "We haven't studied that part of the Civil War yet. Do you think the railroad might have come anywhere near Lewisville?"

"I can't say for sure, but it might have. Your father knows more about this than I do. When he gets home tonight, why don't you ask him? But—until then..." Carol Spencer paused and smiled. "...you could bring that newspaper and come back to the kitchen. Supper won't happen tonight without peeled potatoes!"

Chase's younger sister Sally entered through the back door and joined him and their mother. The three of them worked together to prepare fried chicken, green beans, and potato salad. At 5:15, Chase's father called to say that he would be delayed leaving work. A water pipe had burst in the storeroom of the family's hardware store, and he would need to stay and repair it after the store closed. Carol Spencer filled an extra plate for her husband with the food items from the table. After the meal Chase helped clear the table, dry and put away dishes, and then he went back upstairs to his bedroom.

....

Nearly every night at 8 o'clock, Frank, Griff, and Chase turned on their walkie-talkies to connect with each other. Their conversations were mostly about the things that had happened during their days.

"Are you guys on your radios, yet?" Frank asked, his voice crackling across Griff's and Chase's walkie-talkies a block or two away.

"I'm here," Chase replied.

"Me, too," Griff answered.

"I've been pretty sad that we didn't get to ask Colonel Perkins any of our questions," Frank said.

Griff responded. "Me, too. When I got home, I took a shower, laid down on my bed, closed my eyes, and didn't hear or see *anything* until my dad called me for supper. I guess I was more bushed than I realized!"

"You did a lot today, buddy!" Chase reminded. "No wonder you were so tired. You looked like some sort of superhero when you dove into that water. And when we waded in to meet you, it was a lot colder than I expected. You did *a hero's job* today, Griff!"

"Thanks, Chase, but either one of you would have done the same thing. I was just the closest person to the door when we saw the smoke."

"Speaking of wading in," Frank added, "after church and lunch tomorrow, would you guys care to go back to Mr. Rigsby's house with me? I found out that Colonel Perkins is leaving town on the 7 AM train, so we've missed our chance to talk with him. Mr. Rigsby is the only other person we know who might have answers. We still haven't gotten to ask him about that door on the riverbank. We could meet up at my house and go see him right after lunch."

"I'm good with that," Chase agreed.

"Count me in," Griff responded, "but what does that have to do with 'wading in'?"

Frank laughed. "Nothing, really, except that one day I sure want to see what's behind that door. Hey, I can borrow my uncle's waders, and, Chase, with the pair that you already have, maybe we can check it out!"

"That key that we found in the grandfather clock," Griff began, "I've been thinking that it might fit that lock on the door. Chase, you said it felt like an old padlock, right?"

"Yeah, and you might actually be onto something," Chase commented excitedly. "It makes a lot of sense. Of course, we have to get permission, but I would love to go back there and see if that black key opens the lock! Hey, listen to this. This afternoon I was looking through a book that came in the mail to my dad. My mom told me about how back in the Civil War, when slaves were trying to get to their freedom, they sometimes used the North Star kinda like their compass. As long as they could see that star, they knew by walking toward it they were headed away from slavery and in the direction to find their freedom."

"Chase, that fits the first line of the riddle," Griff proposed happily. *"The star will lead the longing heart.* Guys, we might crack this riddle before much longer!"

....

On Sunday morning Frank noticed Mr. Rigsby in his pew across the aisle at church, and after the service ended, the two of them spoke. He said that the boys were welcome to drop by anytime in the afternoon. Once the three friends had eaten their lunches, Griff, Frank, and Chase met at the end of Frank's driveway. It was two blocks to Mr. Rigsby's place, so they began walking and were on the sidewalk in front of his home by 1:30.

Leonard Rigsby was seated on his front porch swing as the three friends climbed the steps that led from the sidewalk to the brown-brick, three-story home. Except for his navy trousers and brown shoes, the Sunday edition of the Lewisville Ledger hid the rest of the small man. When he heard their footfalls, he lowered the newspaper and peered over its top. "Come on up! Come up and join me!" he offered with his usual, wide smile. "I was just enjoying this brisk weather and reading an article about Colonel Meade's visit yesterday. Come along, and we can go inside."

Mr. Rigsby stood and began to shuffle toward the front door. He spoke over his shoulder. "I planned to be at his presentation yesterday for the meeting of the Historical Society. I didn't attend after all because I have been getting over a cough. But I'm glad to report I am much improved since then." He laughed to himself, folded his newspaper, and motioned them through the open door. The three friends and their host seated themselves around the breakfast table in the kitchen.

Frank spoke first. "Mr. Rigsby, when we were here the other day, there were a few things that we didn't have a chance to ask you. Last weekend when the guys and I took a group of Cub Scouts to clean up the Meade property and the waterline next to the place, Chase saw an old door that was set into the levee at the river bank."

Chase quickly added, "It was a metal door, and it was mostly underwater. I was wearing waders and got close enough to touch a padlock. Everything about it seemed really old."

"I remember that door," he replied thoughtfully and with a slight smile. "When we were children, we used to play in the vineyard. That entire area of the levee sloped from the grand lawn of the home to the New Haven River. As long as I've known about it, that door has been locked-up tight."

Griff stirred anxiously in his chair, waiting for a pause to speak. As the kindly man finished, Griff reached into a front pocket and pulled out a folded sheet of paper. "Mr. Rigsby, Frank mentioned that he started to tell you about the wooden discs, and then you needed to answer a phone call. But since we found them that night, we discovered something else that we think might be connected to them. This was hand-written on the bottom of the box:

Star will lead the longing heart

Earth doth guide the eye

Water proves the promised (there's a word missing)

Word and key disclose

That missing word is faded pretty bad. I've been thinking a lot about this," Griff continued, "so, see if this makes any sense to you. The star in the first line could be Polaris. It's the North Star. It's the direction someone would travel to get to the free states. *Earth* and the *eye* could be talking about the things you'd see along the way. I'm a little stuck on this third line, especially because a word is missing."

"Just a minute, Griff." An expression of deep thought filled Mr. Rigsby's face. He raised his eyes to a bookshelf in an adjoining room beyond his three visitors. He stood, shuffled toward the shelves, and reached for a single book. He removed the small book with its cracked, leather cover, and returned to his seat at the table. He then slowly thumbed through the delicate and yellowed pages. He stopped and studied one page—a page with a penciled image in the margin. Carefully the elderly gentleman rotated the book on the table in the boys' direction. As he scanned their eager faces, he announced, "I've been thinking about what Frank mentioned the other night. Did those discs you saw look anything like this?"

....

BACK TO THE RIVERBANK

CHAPTER 9

The pencil drawing was very familiar to the boys, and they traded excited glances. *"Yes! That's what we saw!"* Griff placed his finger on the page. "This drawing even shows those little holes in the middle of the disc—right there!"

"What are these things, Mr. Rigsby?" Frank asked. "Are they some sort of a coin?"

"They aren't coins, Frank, and I don't know exactly how they were used, but I'm fairly certain those discs, or, as I would call them, tokens, are from the middle part of the 1800s. Let me do more research. I'll place a call to a friend at Midstate University and let you know if I learn anything."

"Gee, thanks, Mr. Rigsby," Chase replied excitedly.

Frank spoke next. "We need to head out now and go to the Meade place so we can get our bikes. We left them there because Griff's dad drove us home after the boat fire."

"Yes, I heard about the excitement yesterday. I am very proud of the three of you. And, Griff, did I understand that you *jumped* in the river?"

"Actually, we *all* went into the water. It was pretty cold, but it felt great to be able to help the people who were in trouble."

Frank stood, and the other boys followed him. "Thank you for letting us come over, Mr. Rigsby. If you learn anything more about those discs, we'd love to hear about it!"

....

It was a fifteen-minute walk from Leonard Rigsby's house on Goldstone Lane to Meade Manor. As they turned onto Wellington Drive, in the distance, two bells rang out from the clock tower above City Hall. When the second peal faded, Frank said, "We don't have any idea if we can get back by the river in another week, and I don't want to put off checking about that door any longer. How do you guys feel about stopping by my house? I can grab the waders I borrowed from my uncle, and, Chase, we can go by your house so you can get yours, too."

"It sounds like a good plan to me. We still have plenty of daylight," Chase agreed.

"Both of you grab your flashlights when we stop," Griff suggested. "I have mine in my pocket. Do either one of you have any waterproof matches?"

"I have a watertight box with a couple of candles and some of those matches," Chase replied. "I'll bring them."

....

As they reached the iron gate and sidewalk that led to the Meade house, their bicycles weren't anywhere in sight— certainly not where they had left them.

"I hope that someone put our bikes in a safe place," Griff commented.

"I'm sure they're fine," Frank insisted. "Hey, that looks like Mr. Lucius, and he's headed this way!" He pointed to a figure fifty yards away walking around the side of the house. The Meade house sat atop a small hill, and the man was approaching from behind it.

"I don't think that's Mr. Lucius, Frank," Chase pointed out as he waved one arm above his head. "Hellooooo."

The fellow looked toward the boys and raised a hand to wave back. He changed his path and began to walk in their direction. The boys continued toward the side of the house and met him there. It was the grandson, Cyrus.

"Hello again!" the fellow answered.

"We were here yesterday visiting with Colonel Meade, and..."

"And you've come back for your bicycles."

"Yes, please," Griff said.

"Those are nice bikes you boys have! My grandfather and I made sure they were stored away safe. They're out back in the shed. Nobody has bothered them. Come with me." Cyrus Evans turned and motioned for them to follow him.

"We really appreciate that," Chase said. Both Chase and Frank placed their waders on the ground and hurried to catch up with the young man. The four of them walked in silence down the hill at the rear of the house. After a moment, Chase spoke again. "We met your grandfather when we came yesterday. He seems like a very nice man."

"He is that," Cyrus replied. "He raised me just like he was my daddy." Following several seconds of silence while they walked, he continued. "We live in a cabin in the back part of the property. It's the only home I've ever had." He reached down and plucked a single blade of tall grass. Cyrus continued walking as he played with it using two fingers, then tossed it aside. "Your bikes are right over there." He pointed to a small barn thirty yards away. Its weathered, red-painted doors were propped open—one of the doors held by a wooden barrel and the other one by a large rock. "There's my granddaddy now."

Stepping through the open doors was the gentleman they met when they arrived to visit with Colonel Meade. This time, instead of wearing an ill-fitting tuxedo, he wore patched overalls, a red plaid shirt, and work boots.

"Welcome back, young fellas. Cyrus and I were just organizing things here in this shed. We may need to be shutting down this farm sooner than later. I've been sorting out what we might be able to sell and what we need to throw away."

Griff was visibly surprised upon hearing this. "Are you saying that you're leaving? Miss Lillian is selling Meade Manor?"

"We hope not, but things aren't looking so good." They entered the barn. "I don't know how much longer Miss Lillian can keep this place. Just about everything here needs fixing. We need to dig a new well. The roof on the main house leaks. She says that her money has almost run out. She used to pay me a little something now and then for the things I do. She used to pay Cyrus, too, but she had to quit that a while back."

"That's terrible," Griff agreed. "It's such a great house—and the property..."

Lucius Evans interrupted, "We were hoping that we could get the house listed with the government. They sometimes sign up a house because of all the history it has. This whole place has had a lot of important things go on over the years, but she hasn't been able to get them to notice us. Miss Lillian was hoping that the colonel could help, but he said he couldn't do anything, either. I jus' wish there was something Cyrus and I could do to help out. She's a proud woman, Miss Lillian, and she doesn't have anything to fall back on if we can't keep this house runnin'."

Each of the boys walked their bicycles out of the storage barn. Nothing was spoken for several seconds, and Frank broke the silence. "We're sorry to know about the troubles here, but we've been wondering something. What about that door on the river—the one that goes into the levee over there?" Frank pointed into the distance. "Do you know much about it—what's in there?"

"What I know is it's been locked up tight and mostly underwater ever since I have lived on the property, and that'll be seventy-five years next month," Mr. Evans volunteered proudly. "We all used to play around there, and we'd call it 'the jail.' I don't think anybody knows what's behind that door. I asked my daddy back then, and he couldn't tell me."

"We were here a week ago on Saturday, and we cleaned up some of the property so people could use that part of the lawn to watch the parade," Chase explained. "We'd like to go back over there and take another look before we leave, if that would be okay."

Griff quickly added, "When we were helping move some furniture for the painting inside, we saw a key. Do you think you could check and see if it would be all right for us to borrow it for a few minutes?"

"Miss Lillian left a little while ago, but it's okay with me. I don't think she'd mind."

As the four of them began to climb the hill toward the house, Mr. Evans continued. "The government place that registers the houses, if they give you a special paper, that means you can get help from the bank to fix up your house. That's what we need. We need some help."

At the back door of the main house, Mr. Lucius looked at Griff and asked, "Do you know where that key is?"

"I do. I'll be right back, guys," Griff said. The two of them entered the house.

A moment later, Griff appeared at the screen door, grinning and holding the rusty iron key. He turned to Mr. Evans and announced, "We'll bring this back soon." Griff joined the friends, and they walked their bicycles into the front yard and onto the sidewalk. There they lowered the kickstands. "Let's do this!" Griff exclaimed.

....

Frank and Chase sat on the grass a few feet from the river, removed their shoes, and eased their legs into the rubber waders. Griff stood between his two friends, and when they were ready, he extended both of his arms and gripped one hand of both Frank and Chase to help them stand.

"Look!" Frank pointed to charred wood against the bank. "There are some pieces of the boat that caught on fire. The current of the river must have caught them and kept them here against the shore. We can at least clean those up before we leave."

Holding the iron key, Chase followed Frank into the river, and in a moment, they stood in waist-high water in front of the old, wood-framed metal door.

"I see what you mean now," Frank marveled. "This looks like the kind of door that would lead you into a dungeon or something."

"We need to get closer," Chase proposed. "The lock is down below where you can't see it—you can only feel it."

With much effort, they both forced their way through the thick willows and reeds. Chase lowered his hand into the murky river water and gripped the padlock. "Here goes!" he spoke loud enough for both boys to hear. At first, the key would not go into the keyhole. Layers of sediment kept him from inserting it. But after scraping the lock, on his second try, it dropped perfectly into the opening of the padlock. With considerable effort, the key finally turned, and the bottom half of the lock swung open. *"We got it!"* Chase yelled. *"It's open!"* He removed the antique padlock from the hasp and held it above his head.

"Is there a doorknob on it?" Griff asked from the shore. "Can you see any way to pull it open?"

Chase tossed the lock and key to Griff, then put both of his hands underwater again and felt the area where the padlock had been. "There's a handle. I don't feel anything like a doorknob, but there's a big, metal handle."

"You realize, don't you," Frank began, "that if there's not an equal amount of water behind the door inside that room, we'll never be able to pull it open. The water pressure on our side will be too much."

"Let's hope that there's *some* water back there—but not *too* much," Chase ventured. "Come over here by me and grab onto the handle, and we can both pull." Frank pushed in close to his friend and reached into the murky water with Chase to grip the door handle.

"Ready?" Chase asked. "Let's pull on three—with everything you've got! One...two...*three!*" The door didn't budge. It seemed impossibly stuck—as if it was welded shut. "Again! One...two...*three!*" Nothing moved.

"Set your feet and lean back when you pull!" Griff suggested from the riverbank.

"This is it! I *know* it is." Chase insisted. Ready? One...two...*THREE!*"

The door, which had been closed and locked for at least seventy-five years, came open a mere inch. The expressions on Chase's and Frank's face told Griff all that he needed to know. *"You got it? Is it open?"* Griff asked anxiously.

"It's *starting* to open," Frank acknowledged. "Come on, Chase—put everything you have into it this time! One...two...*THREE!*"

Bubbles of air rose to the water surface in front of them as the door groaned open another six inches. After two more tugs, it was ajar enough so a person could squeeze through the opening.

Griff paced on the grass of the levee. "Okay, guys, you *gotta* tell me what you can see. I *can't stand* not being down there with you!"

Frank pulled his penlight from his shirt pocket, switched it on, and leaned his head and shoulders through the opening. He said nothing for fifteen seconds and then stepped back into the daylight. Chase and Griff stared at him and waited for him to speak. *"Well?"* Chase asked.

"It's got bricks on all of the sides. The ceiling of it is kinda rounded. The water inside ends after about ten feet and the back of it slopes up. Guys, it's not a room. *It's a tunnel!*

. . . .

CLUES IN THE CELLAR

CHAPTER 10

"A *tunnel*? To *where*?" Griff asked. "What would it be for?"

"I wanna check it out," Chase declared. "We've gotten this far. We *can't* just close it up and walk away now!"

"Well, I want to know where it goes, too, but we need to be smart, and we need to ask permission," Frank replied. "Chase, did you see that rope back in the barn? There was a good size length of it hanging by the door. I noticed it when we were leaving. It was about as thick as a clothesline. I'd feel better about going into the tunnel if we could pull one end of a rope with us."

"I'll go back and look for it," Griff offered. "If I see Mr. Lucius, I'll ask permission, but if not, I'll borrow it and we can put it back when we're finished."

While Griff was away, Frank and Chase exchanged guesses concerning the purpose of the tunnel. Who built it? When? And why? Why didn't anybody seem to know about it?

Griff returned to the river out of breath. "I saw Mr. Lucius, and he said it would be okay. Here's one end. I'll unroll the rope to you from up on the levee when you go inside."

Chase and Frank pulled the door open several more

inches. This let them pass through the opening with their shoulders barely touching the edges. "If you don't hear from us in ten minutes," Frank proposed as his head disappeared from view, "find a phone and call your dad!"

Griff sat on the ground with the rope in his lap. As the boys progressed further into the tunnel, he unwound a few feet at a time toward the open doorway. At times there was no movement for a half-minute or longer, and then without warning, all of the slack would be pulled tight. Griff guessed that the full length of the rope measured two-hundred feet. Five minutes passed, then ten. When his friends stopped pulling on it, he estimated there was just twenty feet of rope remaining in his lap.

Above the gentle sounds of water lapping at the bank, he began to hear faint voices. Then, in the minute that followed, the muffled, echoing tones of Chase and then Frank grew louder through the tunnel door. Griff stood and waited.

The top of Chase's head and then his shoulders appeared. When he was entirely out of the opening, he turned around, looked at Griff, and then instructed, "Tie a knot where your end of the rope went through the door. We need to stretch it across the yard and see how far it goes toward the house."

"So—what did you see?" Griff asked as he added a butterfly knot to the rope. "What was in there?"

Once Frank followed Chase through the iron door, they both waded back to the bank and stepped onshore. "It's empty as far as we can tell," Frank replied. "At the end— well, as far as we could go—was a wooden door about five feet tall. It felt pretty solid, and it moved just a little when I pushed on it. There was no handle, so it's probably either stuck or locked from the other side."

"And except for a little jog to the left about halfway into it, the whole tunnel was as straight as an arrow," Chase reported. He sat on the ground and began to pull his waders off. Frank did the same thing.

"Here's the knot," Griff announced, holding it for the other boys to see. "So, you're saying that the tunnel heads toward the house?"

"Yep," Frank replied. "I'll hold the knot here near the door, and you two start walking and stretch it out. That little jog was probably just about where the hedgerow is, so Chase, you bend the angle just a couple of degrees left at that point, and we'll see where the rope runs out."

As Griff and Chase walked away from the river, they pulled the rope with them up the levee. At the hedge, they carried the rope through and continued moving toward the house. It was no surprise to either of them that the rope almost exactly reached the foundation of the main house. They grinned at each other and turned around to retrace their steps and meet up again with Frank. Griff gathered the rope into loops as they walked.

Chase spoke. "I don't know what all of this means, but the next thing we *have* to do is talk to Miss Lillian!"

"I agree. With all of the history of this house and the fact that no one—not even Mr. Evans, who is seventy-five—knows what the tunnel is for, we *have* to keep exploring!"

"You're right," Chase agreed. "Somewhere down in the cellar of that house is probably at least *part* of the answer to the mystery. I just hope we can get in there and look."

Frank approached them from the riverbank holding onto the knotted end of the rope. "What did you two find out?"

"It's just like you guessed," Griff noted. "The rope reached exactly to the edge of the house. The other side of the wooden door you guys found must lead into the cellar. What I can't wait to find out is why! *Why* the tunnel and *why* the door?"

Lucius Evans came through a gap in the hedge. "Did you boys find what you were looking for?" he asked. "Did the rope help?"

"Yes, it did, Mr. Evans," Griff replied. "Thank you for letting us borrow it."

"Please just call me Lucius. Everybody does."

"We feel terrible to think that you may have to leave the place where you and your family grew up," Frank said.

He smiled. "Thank you, son. Walk with me. I want to show you something." He reached out a calloused hand, and Griff gave the rope to the gray-haired grandfather. Lucius turned and led the way back through the hedge. They walked toward the rear of the house, and then he turned away from it onto a well-worn path. Fifty yards later the trail continued and meandered through bushes and trees. After several minutes on the path, they reached a clearing. At its far edge was a simple log cabin. Gray smoke rose from its chimney into the cloudless, blue sky.

"This place is where I was born. It's where my daddy was born, and most of my family before him." He continued on the path and finally climbed the two steps of the cabin's porch. He pushed open the door and stepped aside so the boys could enter. "Come in."

The one-room cabin was teeming with the aroma of something savory being warmed. The boys could see the pot hanging above glowing logs in the fireplace. "Cyrus is out chopping firewood right now, but here's what I wanted to show you." He pointed to a simple picture frame hanging on the wall at shoulder height. It held a piece of glass pressed against a yellowed document. "Step up close, boys. I want you to see this. Would one of you read the words out loud?"

Frank was the closest. He looked at Chase and Griff, turned to face the handwritten words, cleared his throat, and began.

Deed Of Manumission

To all whom these presents, greetings. I, Charles Meade, of the County of Jeffers, for every good cause and consideration hereby declare free, manumit, and enfranchise the following person, to wit a man age twenty-six named Isaac Evans to be set at liberty on the third day of July 1862. I discharge from all claim and right of property whatsoever from my heirs or any other person claiming him in manner and form.

Witness my hand and seal on this second day of July in the year of our Lord 1858.

Frank stepped away from the document and turned to his

friends. Lucius Evans' face beamed. Griff and Chase were speechless.

"You see, boys, I am a descendant of Isaac Evans, *that* freed man. This paper tells me so. My great-granddaddy was set free by Mr. Charles Meade, and years later, my granddaddy was born free. Both of them could have left this house and gone to another place north of here to do anything they wanted to do. But they stayed here because the Meade family *loved* my family—my people. This was their home, and they treated them right even before that paper was written. They treated them right until the day they died. I expected that one day I would be buried out there next to my kin." Lucius pointed to a window. "But I guess that won't happen now."

The boys exchanged glances. "Because Miss Lillian might have to move away?" Griff asked.

"You say she wants her house to be recognized as a historic home?" Chase questioned.

"That's what I meant to say," Mr. Evans replied. "If we had one of those special signs, Miss Lillian said we could afford to fix things, and we could let people come and visit inside and see that great, old house."

All of the boys had the same thought. Chase looked at the others, his eyes wide with excitement. "Mr. Lucius, do you think it would be okay if we went into the cellar for a few minutes? We have an idea about something, but we need to get down there to be sure."

"Miss Lillian is still gone, so come with me. I'll take you there myself."

The four of them retraced their steps through the field and trees to the rear of the house. "There's some cellar doors over there by the back steps," Mr. Evans pointed to double doors set at a forty-five degree angle against the base of the house. "If it's okay with you, I'll stay up here while you boys go down. My old knees don't do so good on stairs anymore."

Griff and Frank pulled the two doors open. The hinges creaked as they laid them back on both sides of the opening. The damp smells from beneath the house of earth, stone, and mildew filled their nostrils. Chase pulled his penlight from a front jeans pocket. "There's a switch on the wall for the lights," Mr. Evans explained. "When you reach the last step, it'll be on the left."

"Thank you. We won't be down there long," Griff replied.

....

When the three friends reached the bottom step, they paused for their eyes to adjust to the dim surroundings. Two dusty and bare lightbulbs hanging from the ceiling, thirty feet apart, were only slightly helpful as the boys surveyed the setting filled with trunks and crates. Stacks of old furniture, a wagon wheel, a dressmaker's dummy, steamer trunks, and boxes of wood and cardboard as high as the boys' shoulders created a maze of paths that turned left, then right, and eventually led back to the cellar steps.

Griff stretched his full height and held the flashlight above his head. He pointed it in the direction of the end of the house that faced the river. Griff strained to see into the distance. "Over on that far wall I can see some kind of a big cabinet in the middle of it. Help me move this trunk and these boxes, and I think we can get back there to it."

With a path barely two feet wide among decades of stored belongings, the boys finally shifted enough things to squeeze into the far end of the cellar. "I'm thinking that the other side of this cabinet lines up with the tunnel," Chase ventured.

Frank nodded in agreement. "Let's try to move it away from the wall. If we can slide the cabinet just a couple of inches, I can shine my light behind it. Both of you—get your hands into this space and let's all pull."

After being unable to get more than the tips of fingers between the cabinet and the wall, and nearly exhausting themselves with no success, they stepped back.

"Maybe this thing is fastened to the ground," Frank offered.

Griff knelt on the damp floor and opened the two front doors in the bottom part of the cabinet. "And just *maybe* I can move these jars and reach the back of it to see what's there." He handed at least two dozen dusty and empty canning jars to Chase and Frank. They placed them on the floor out of the way. Griff pushed his upper body into the emptied cabinet and thumped forcefully on the rear panel. He let out a howl! *"The back of this thing is false! It's on a hinge! It pushed open, and right here is the wooden door that you two saw from the tunnel!"*

He backed out of the cabinet and placed one hand on the floor to help him stand. Instead of touching the floor, his hand came down on a cold object in the form of a garden hose. Instinctively Griff withdrew his hand, but not before he felt its scales. *It was without question a snake!*

WORD AND KEY DISCLOSE

CHAPTER 11

For several seconds, Griff froze in silence. Not only was it dark, but he also didn't know which part of the snake his hand touched, or what kind of snake he had encountered.

"Guys, get back—quick! I'm pretty sure I just found a snake!"

"Where?" Frank asked anxiously.

There was scarcely any room to back away from the area without stepping on the shoes of the person behind him. They all moved clear of the front of the cabinet.

Frank stood on his tiptoes and shined his light on the floor. "I see it! Yeah, it's looking right at me. We're okay, guys. It's a rat snake, so we're safe. They're actually good to have around *if* you can get over the creepiness. They eat mice."

"You're right," Griff confirmed. "I'll bet it's down here getting ready to brumate for the winter. I think I can use my shoe to help him to move along somewhere else." He chuckled, and nudged the snake with the toe of his sneaker. With hardly a sound, it slithered away into the darkness.

"Okay, back to the business at hand," a relieved Griff directed. Both friends took turns observing the false door in the back of the cabinet.

Chase's expression brightened as he announced, "The faded part of the riddle on the box of discs must be the word *door*! *Water proves the promised door!* The word *proves* can mean *reveals*. It is all starting to make sense now!"

"*Boys! Boys!*" It was the anxious voice of Lucius Evans. "Would you come up here?"

Frank turned toward the cellar door and cupped his hands to his mouth. "We'll be there in a minute!"

"I wonder what's up," Griff said as he dusted off his knees and shirt. They retraced their path through the stacked boxes, old furniture, and wooden crates. In a moment, they reached the stone steps and climbed into the daylight.

"Miss Lillian called on the telephone to see if you boys were still here."

Frank, Griff, and Chase looked at each other, confused by his words.

"She has been at Mr. Rigsby's house, and both of them are on the way back here. She said for me to tell you not to leave."

....

The three boys closed and latched the double cellar doors. Mr. Evans went inside the house. None of the friends spoke as they walked around to the front of Meade Manor and sat on the porch steps. In front of them were their three bicycles and the two sets of waders. They stared down the sidewalk, past the gate, and onto the road. Each person tried to imagine what was about to happen.

"Do you think we did something that we weren't supposed to?" Chase asked.

Griff replied. "Well, we asked for permission to use the key and go in the tunnel."

"*And* to go into the cellar," Griff added. "I don't know what might have made her upset."

The sunlight glinted off the distant windshield of a vehicle as it entered the road far from the house. In silence, the three friends focused on the lone car as it grew larger, finally reached the gravel entrance to Meade Manor, then turned onto the horseshoe-shaped driveway. The dark blue sedan came to a stop in front of the house. As the boys stood and began to walk toward it, Miss Lillian opened the driver's door and stepped out. Wisps of windblown hair framed her pale face. She wore a flowing, white dress with sleeves that extended past her hands, appearing the perfect matron of the place that she had always called home.

Leonard Rigsby emerged from the far side of the car. He lowered his cane, walked carefully around behind it, and shuffled toward the waiting boys.

"Young men!" Miss Lillian began to speak as she approached the boys. They braced themselves for a harsh rebuke. "What you have done..." She paused again, adding drama to the moment, "...is nothing short of remakable! You probably have just saved Meade Manor from being lost by my family for-evah. You may have helped to preserve this historic house for future generations."

The astonishment on the faces of the Bon Air boys was evident to all.

"What Miss Lillian is saying," Mr. Rigsby explained, "is we think that finding the wooden tokens may be a discovery sufficient to have this house and land declared a historic location in the national registry. If we can please all go inside, I believe I can explain."

Lucius Evans appeared on the front porch when the car arrived. He supported the arm of Miss Lillian and walked with her onto the porch and through the door. Frank and Griff assisted Mr. Rigsby, and in a moment, they were all seated in the parlor.

"Where are the tokens, Frank?" Mr. Rigsby asked. "Let me see them, please."

Chase and Frank went to the bookshelf at the end of the room. Chase brought a nearby footstool to the base of the shelves. Frank climbed it and retrieved the wooden box. He handed it to Mr. Rigsby.

"After you visited me earlier today, I conducted more research about these, and I placed a long-distance phone call to my friend at Midstate University." Leonard Rigsby paused and examined one of the discs. "After that conversation, I phoned Miss Lillian and invited her over to share the news. These discs are almost unknown to most historians. They are practically legendary to those who study slavery and the abolitionist movement. *These tokens are handmade buttons!* Each of them contains descriptions about specific stations on a line of the underground railroad. The symbols on the tokens reveal where to find a station—each one a hiding place hosted by a sympathetic man or woman or family—a safe place for a night offering shelter and food on the pathway headed north."

Frank glanced at Miss Lillian and noticed that her face was beaming with delight. Mr. Rigsby continued.

"A slave who wanted to gain his or her freedom would find someone in the movement at the southern side of the underground railroad. That unnamed person provided a set of five or six or seven of these buttons to that slave. Buttons on the clothes of slaves a hundred years ago were mostly crude and simple, so these wooden ones would not have attracted any attention. The plain side was sewn facing forward. The side with the symbols and details that led to the next stop on the railroad—that side was sewn toward the clothes with the first station as the top button and progressing down from there. If a slave was ever caught carrying a map or any written directions, well, that sort of thing could compromise the identity of everyone along the line. However, these buttons were foolproof— and they did their job perfectly! It was one of the best-kept secrets of the abolitionist movement!"

Miss Lillian added, "I always felt that this house was one of the stations on the railroad, but I didn't have any evidence of this."

Mr. Rigsby began again. "Different lines of the railroad used different methods. Only a few of them used buttons, but along each route, the slaves seeking their freedom met good people who would hide them, feed them, care for their injuries or sicknesses, and then send them to the next station. These buttons acted as *passwords* at each station. A button was proof to the stationmaster—just like a secret password—that the traveler was truly fleeing slavery and not acting as a bounty hunter for the slaveowners. My research shows that when they reached the station at the end of this line, just before crossing into a free state, they were supplied with one new set of clothes. In that exchange, the slaves gave up these buttons. Meade Manor was no doubt one of the final stations for *many dozens, perhaps hundreds,* of slaves. Those tokens—those buttons that you found—they are how we can be *confident* that this house played a vital part in helping people transition from bondage to freedom."

"I can hardly believe it!" Chase exclaimed. "We were just helping Donnie when we found them, so *he* is the reason that we were here at all!"

"And even before we discovered the discs, we found that old door that leads into the levee," Griff added, and then he turned to Miss Lillian. "We noticed it when we were cleaning up along the water for the boat parade."

Leonard Rigsby looked at them with a puzzled expression. "Do you mean that locked room by the riverbank?"

"Wait until you see it!" Frank exclaimed. "It's not a room, Mr. Rigsby. *It's a tunnel!* And it leads under the levee to a hidden door behind a cabinet down in the cellar!"

Miss Lillian gasped, then managed a wide smile. Mr. Rigsby leaned forward in his chair.

"Oh my goodness, Lillian! With both of these discoveries,

I am *positive* that the National Historic Site commission will approve your home! That tunnel was most certainly placed there for northbound slaves. I have no doubt that scores of them used it to enter this house for food and comfort offered by your ancestors. They would have left here from it for their final path to freedom across the river!"

Miss Lillian stood and motioned for the boys to come close. With her arms outstretched, she took a hand of Frank and Griff in hers and smiled at each of them. "You will nev-ah know how thankful I am for what you have done for me, and for what I hope are hundreds of people who will visit and learn about this wonderful old house."

"We didn't do anything, really," Chase responded. "We just let our curiosity take over."

Griff added laughing, "Even though *sometimes* our curiosity takes us to strange places!"

Suddenly the grandfather clock on the stairway landing struck the hour: *bong, bong, bong, bong, bong.* Chase, Frank, and Griff smiled at each other. Only *they* understood the significance of those chimes. Before anyone else spoke, all of them heard footsteps on the front porch. The door swung open, and Cyrus Evans appeared in the entrance to the parlor. He held something in his hand. "Excuse me," he said. "I just found this under the bushes by the porch and it looks like there's quite a bit of money inside. Did any of you lose a wallet?"

"*We* didn't," Griff answered, "but I'm pretty sure we know the guy that *did!*" He and the other Bon Air boys burst into laughter!

A FEW MORE THOUGHTS

Lucius and Cyrus Evans were faithful workers who helped Miss Lillian keep Meade Manor operating. They lovingly did this even when she was no longer able to pay them. They served Miss Lillian because they cared about her and the place they all called home.

In the Bible, in the book of James chapter 1, the writer calls himself a servant of God. We don't see many people today who identify themselves as 'servants.' The dictionary defines a servant as "a devoted and helpful follower or supporter." Sometimes a wealthy person might employ devoted helpers such as maids, butlers, gardeners, or a chauffeur to drive them in a fancy car.

A servant can choose each day between doing his job or leaving to go somewhere else for a different job that is easier or more satisfying. A slave, on the other hand, is bound (tied) to his master. He cannot leave. He or she doesn't have the same choices. Those who are slaves must do what their masters say.

You might be thinking, "Wait a minute! There is no such thing as slavery or slaves today! We fought a war under President Abraham Lincoln to be sure slaves were freed!" If you believe that all slavery ended then you would be partly right and partly wrong. You see, this very day there are many people all around us who are slaves. Oh, they don't have visible chains on their ankles. No one forces them to work in the hot sun. Instead of those things, we see people who are "chained" to drugs, alcohol, and other unhealthy things. These "slaves" might look like everyday people—possibly ones you know—but they are unable to free themselves by their own efforts from these actions and patterns.

In Romans 6:16, the writer tells us, "Whatever you serve becomes your master." The verse doesn't say *whoever* you serve becomes your master. The word in the verse is *whatever*. This tells us that *things, actions, and attitudes* can control people and trap them into a life that is much like being in a prison.

What can a person do to become free and leave that kind of life? There *is* a way to escape slavery, and it doesn't require you to travel on the underground railroad. It happens when people choose to turn from their old habits and let God become the loving Master in their life, heart, and mind. That type of commitment is what a bondservant looks like. God then "writes" His name permanently on the bondservant. He commits Himself to them and they commit themselves to Him for all time!

Read the words of Jesus in John 15:15: "No longer do I call you a servant because a servant isn't able to know what his master does: but I call you my friends, and everything that I hear from God I will tell you."

Everyone serves someone or something, whether it is for good or for bad. As slaves to sin, we don't have any power. As servants of God, we have all power to overcome the evil around us.

....

Be sure to enjoy all of the
Bon Air Boys Adventures

The Secret Of Hickory Hill
Lights On Wildcat Mountain
Whispers In The Wind
(and others)
available from Amazon.com

Also available
as Kindle E-Books

Stay connected with
The Bon Air Boys
and the author by visiting
BonAirBoys.com
There you will find the latest information
about upcoming books and products.